FAVOR FOR A FRIEND
The Funny Detective – Volume 6

David Berardelli

FAVOR FOR A FRIEND
The Funny Detective – Volume 6

FICTION4ALL

Chapter 1

The morning started off just like any other summer morning in Central Florida. Bright and sunny, the thermometer already nudging closer and closer to eighty degrees, and with just a few strings of clouds drifting lazily in the sky.

I woke at around eight—my usual wakeup time nowadays. Like most folks, I'd come to realize the hard way that by the time one reaches the unpleasant age of forty, he fully understands that his chances of saving the world by getting up disgustingly early are slim at best, and that the world will go on as usual, no matter what time of day it happens to be.

After a shower and a shave, I shuffled into the kitchen in my bathrobe, and was in the process of making coffee when the doorbell buzzed.

I immediately spun around and gawked at the front door as if some hideous monster from a horror flick was about to burst in and select me for its breakfast snack.

Being a private eye for the last decade and a half, I'd become more than slightly suspicious by nature. And when someone buzzes your doorbell at eight-thirty in the morning, red flags automatically go up, your head begins to spin, and you find yourself wondering who in blazes could be standing on your front stoop.

I haven't gotten the morning paper for years, so I knew for a fact that a paperboy wasn't standing around out there, waiting to be paid for my subscription. And the mail didn't usually arrive at the complex until after ten o'clock. Besides, I wasn't expecting anything from the postman—at least not for the next hour and a half.

Uneasy and somewhat flustered, I checked the wall clock in the living room to make sure I wasn't hallucinating. It wasn't that I was shitfaced from having spent the previous night at some wild party—although I wouldn't have minded being invited to one of those once in a while. But when you find yourself rapidly approaching the dreaded halfway point that separates forty from fifty, you realize that most of the fun things in your life are now behind you, and that everything else has become nothing more than wishful thinking. I'd spent the previous night quietly, as usual, and after yet one more in a long string of uneventful weekends, discovered once again that life may not have begun at forty, but it sure as hell felt like it had ended—or at least tapered off—at that cursed age.

Even so, my hackles were up, and my defense mechanism was already switched to the *on* mode. Before tiptoeing to the front door, I grabbed my trusty Cheetah .380, which I kept hidden underneath a dishtowel on the sink counter. For emergencies, of course. I didn't expect trouble at such an early hour, but a private detective quickly learns early on in his career how easy it is to make enemies, and that

6

these fiends seldom care what hour of the day they choose to wreak their vengeance.

Once I reached the door, I peered through the peephole. And sighed in great relief when I saw the figure out there on my front stoop.

Neil Haversack was standing at my front door in his uniform. He looked even more uncomfortable than usual. In fact, I could tell by his body language—and also by the fact that he was glancing in every conceivable direction to see if anyone was watching him—that he really didn't want to be standing where he was.

On impulse, I rubbed my eyes. Then waited for my vision to clear before attempting another peek. It wasn't that I didn't accept what I was looking at. I just decided that I had to make sure that my eyes weren't deceiving me.

The doorbell buzzed again.

I knew right then that I should open the door. Otherwise, Neil would get mad and start pounding. I wasn't ready for something like that. Especially since I hadn't even had my first cup of coffee. Neil was hard to take when things were going smoothly. However, before coffee and breakfast, dealing with him would be like arguing with a wounded bear.

Taking a breath, I slid the chain out of its slot, unlocked the door and pulled it open.

Neil stood there, looking like he was about to explode. The first thing he noticed was the gun in my hand. The second thing he saw was that my robe was partially open. Instead of mentioning the gun or the robe, he just said, "Took ya long enough." Then

7

he bulled his way past me. "By the way, don't shoot me, Deacon. I didn't come here to die. And close that damn robe. I'm not in the mood for laughs this early in the morning."

He was checking out my apartment as I closed the door. I fastened my robe and realized that he was actually standing in my living room. Neil had been here before, but under much different circumstances. And it had been quite a while ago. He just wasn't the chummy type who went around, visiting his buds in his spare time. Especially so early in the morning.

This told me something bad—or very important—was up.

When I found my voice, I said, "Morning, Neil…"

"Yeah. Whatever." He glanced toward the kitchen and sniffed. "Coffee made yet?"

"It should be ready any second. Have a seat." I gestured to the couch.

He grumbled something incomprehensible and sat down. I couldn't help noticing how uncomfortable he looked, sitting there, staring at my TV and stereo setup. He seemed worried that he'd caught me at some inopportune moment. I wanted to tell him I was alone but didn't want to ruin the moment. I discovered that I was really enjoying this. I resisted the overwhelming urge to tell him a local stripper was waiting for me in my bedroom. That would have been cruel. It would have also depressed me later on, when I went back into the

8

bedroom to change clothes and noticed the empty bed.

I figured Neil had come here for something important. Since we'd been friends such a long time, I guessed that he wanted me for something he didn't want to ask anyone else to do. He also knew I'd do whatever he needed done, so I decided to make this a little more challenging for him.

"Nice weather we've been having," I said.

"Cork it, Deacon," he snapped. "I'm not here 'cause I wanna be."

"I figured as much."

"How could you tell?"

I shrugged. "You've never seemed the sort to stop over before work, have some good coffee for a change and chew the fat. Besides, you don't live anywhere near this part of town. This tells me you came here on purpose."

He turned toward the kitchen. "That damn coffee ready yet?"

I got up and went into the kitchen. When I turned to grab a couple of cups from the drainer, I saw that he'd come over and planted his fleshy butt on one of my two barstools on the other side of the open counter.

"It's ready," I said.

He was obviously waiting for me to start pouring. When I didn't move fast enough, he said, "You need an invitation?"

"For what?"

"Deacon, pour me some damn coffee and quit trying to be cute."

I poured two cups and added a sugar cube to mine. Knowing he took his black, I slid it over. He grabbed it, lifted it, and sipped. Then scowled and set it back down on the counter in front of him.

"So...what's going on in your neck of the woods?" I put my cup on the counter. "What's the nature of this mildly pleasant but extremely spontaneous little visit?"

"Cut the crap, Deacon. You know I wouldn't be here if it wasn't important."

"This is important? Really?" I couldn't help myself. "Well, gee golly!"

His glare didn't wane. "You gonna be serious for once? Or do I gotta blow your head off and plead temporary insanity?"

"All righty, then." I took my coffee into the living room and sat on the couch. "Tell me what's going on."

He came over and sat down at the other end. He had another sip from his cup and sat back. "Actually, I need your help."

"See there? That wasn't so hard, was it?"

"Yeah. It was. Damned hard."

"Okay. Now that we've got the damned hard stuff out of the way..." I had more coffee and waited.

"It's like this, Deacon. I need someone I can trust."

"I didn't know you cared."

He ignored that—which told me right then that he was not in his usual quippy mood. "This involves my niece."

10

"Your sister's daughter?"

He glared. "That's what a niece is, isn't it?"

"Well, she could be your *brother's* daughter—"

"I don't have a brother and you know it. Asshole."

"Or maybe, if you take that once-removed crap and stick it in the equation—"

"You can stick yours where the sun don't shine, Deacon…"

"Ouch. Sounds painful."

Neil groaned and rubbed his temples.

Nope, definitely not in the mood for quips.

"Okay, then. Now that we've got the girl's family roots established…"

"Are you gonna shut up and let me tell ya what you need to know?"

"Does this mean you're actually *hiring* me for something?"

"I wouldn'ta come over here for the coffee…"

"It's helluva lot better than that crap you drink all day at the Station."

Neil looked like he'd just smelled something horrible. "This is *flavored,* dammit. It's got *vanilla* in it. Or that fancy shit those damn Brazilians stick in it—"

"It's Swiss mocha. I thought I'd experiment, try something different."

Neil winced and put the cup down. "Now I think I might be sick."

"Don't be silly. Let's get back to the important issue. You're actually hiring me?"

"You could say that."

Something about this didn't make any sense. Neil was a lot of things, but being generous with his money wasn't something he was noted for. This told me that whatever he was involved with was an emergency. "You know how much I charge, don't you?"

"Yeah. I do. But this is my niece we're talking about, now."

"Your sister's daughter."

"I already told ya that. Let's get on with this, all right?"

"I guess we could do that, since you're already here, and haven't come just to chew the fat or drink the bad coffee…"

He sighed. "Like I just said—"

"What's her name?"

"Huh?"

"If this involves your niece, and if you really want me in on this, I think I should know a few incidentals. I'm funny that way. For one thing, it really helps to know the name of the niece of the man who's paying me—"

"Erin, dammit."

I thought that one over. "Her name is Erin Dammit. I see… Is Dammit her middle name? Or—"

"Deacon, you're an asshole."

"Now what does *that* have to do with anything?"

"Just stating a fact. Now…can we please get back to why I'm here? I'm sure you can tell by now that I really don't wanna be here in the first place."

"You've only mentioned that a couple of times before. Besides, I could tell that when I first looked through the peephole and saw you trying to turn into Claude Rains. What's wrong? Is it the neighborhood? The tennis courts overlooking the lake? The fresh air? The strong scent of honeysuckle playing nice with your pheromones?"

He sighed and suddenly looked tired. "Deacon, dammit…"

"Sorry. Go ahead, Neil. Tell me. I promise I'll actually listen this time."

He took a breath and rubbed his temples. Then he sat back and took another breath. "Like I said, this involves Erin, and it's pretty bad."

"How bad is pretty bad?"

"As bad as it gets."

"Then it's much worse than just pretty bad?"

Neil suddenly looked grim. "Someone tried to snatch her. At gunpoint."

Chapter 2

After a quick breakfast, I got in my classic TransAm and drove directly to OPD in downtown Orlando.

My mind had been working nonstop ever since Neil had left my apartment, and I hardly even remembered the drive to the Station.

According to what Neil had told me, his niece, Erin Dobbs, was being held somewhere in Police Headquarters by Detective Miranda Benton, an undercover cop he'd known for several years. Neil had also told me in strict confidence that Benton was one of the few cops he trusted with his niece's life.

"Benton's good," he'd told me back in my apartment. "She's also tough and won't put up with any shit. She'll stay with Erin and won't let anyone talk to her until we get there."

"Just how did this all happen?" I'd asked. "Are drugs involved?"

"Erin's not on drugs." Neil's instant frown suggested that he didn't appreciate the question. "Never has been. I know how that sounds, coming from an uncle, especially since I don't see much of her at all these days. But I'd know. Her mother would have told me. Jane and Erin have been close for years. Erin's not the type to put anything in her body that would hurt her or impede her judgment.

14

She's athletic and has been health-minded since junior high. She was heavy into volleyball and track, even took dancing lessons for three or four years in grade school. She can't stand the taste of alcohol or beer. A glass of wine puts her out like a light."

"Drugs are different," I'd argued.

"She told me she tried weed once at a party and got sick to her stomach. She said she was nauseous for two days. She goes to Rollins, Deacon. She's in her third year. She's got a good head on her shoulders. She's a very smart, sensible girl."

"Lots of women are smart." I hadn't wanted to sound so negative, but since he'd picked me to confide in, I had to put aside our friendship and approach this objectively. "A few of them are even smart and sensible. But that doesn't mean they'll put their intelligence and common sense into high gear when they stumble across some guy with a mouthful of great lines. Hormones always win out, my friend. You know that as well as I do. And that goes for both sexes. We all have our weak spots. Every single one of us."

Neil then told me about some guy Erin had recently hooked up with. He was the guy this entire matter seemed to be all about. Johnny Grayson was his name. Erin had met him at one of the local Winter Park clubs just a few weeks ago. Since Erin was only twenty, she'd borrowed a fake ID from one of her friends so she could join them inside, meet people and dance. She and her girlfriends went to this same place a couple of times before. Erin met

Grayson on the dance floor. He had some good moves, and "a girl her age," as Neil had said, "really goes for a guy with good moves."

"What else does he have?" I'd asked. "Expensive clothes? A fancy ride?"

"She says he's a great dresser and drives a red Vette."

"Old? Or new?"

"Brand-new."

That made me suspicious. "We're talking upwards of sixty or eighty K. Just how old is this character?"

"He told Erin twenty-nine, but she said he looks and acts older. Maybe thirty-two or so."

"That's a lot of jack for a guy that age. Unless the Vette's a lease."

"He told her he bought and paid cash for it."

"Then he's either lying to make himself look good or he's into stolen cars or drugs. Or he could be one of those Internet geeks who turned billionaire by his twentieth birthday."

"She said he's good-looking."

"Geeks are out, then. The ones I've seen actually look like geeks. No, he's definitely into something heavy."

"My thoughts exactly."

"She didn't say anything else about him?"

"Apparently someone's been following her for the last few days. And some asshole in a good suit scared the crap out of her when she went to the Mall with two of her friends. This was what prompted

Jane to call and set me straight about what's going on. And why I'm here with ya right now."

"How'd he scare her?"

"At gunpoint."

"He pointed a *gun* at her?"

"He showed it to her. Casually."

"Her friends see it, too?"

"That's where the story gets a little cloudy."

My suspicions went up again. "What exactly happened?"

"Erin said they'd just walked out of one of the boot outlets when they all decided to visit the ladies' room."

I shook my head. "That never ceases to amaze me."

"Howzat?"

"Women going to the bathroom together."

Neil groaned.

"Doesn't it amaze you?"

"Deacon…"

"Look at it this way and you'll understand where I'm coming from. You and I and some other guy are out doing things together—maybe at the shooting range, or skinning a deer, or perhaps going after wild boars with crossbows. Or maybe we were rock-climbing—"

"Dammit, Deacon…"

"Anyway, I decide I need to use the toilet. Would you and the other guy jump in and say, "Yippie! Let's all go!"? Or would I just wander off into the bushes and—"

"Deacon, shuddup."

17

I shrugged. "Just making a point."

"Make it later. This is serious."

"Then please do go on."

"Like I said, they were all on their way to the ladies' room when this guy suddenly appears."

"Appears? You mean, like a ghost?"

"Don't be stupid. He'd obviously been following them and stepped in front of her before she could follow her friends in."

"Then no one else saw him?"

"Once again, this is where the story gets hazy."

I didn't want Neil to know how suspicious I was of all this. I figured he was suspicious as well, even though his niece was involved. Neil was a cop. A good one. But since this involved his family, he had to tread lightly. And since I was his friend, so did I.

"What happened then?"

"He took her aside and said that she needed to come along with him. He had a few questions to ask her."

"What sort of questions?"

"Didn't say."

"Then he showed her the gun?"

"He made the action really subtle. He had his hand in his jacket pocket and kind of pulled it out an inch or two. Just enough for her to see the piece in the holster attached to his hip."

"Clever. What did she do?"

"Whaddya think? She got scared."

"She run?"

18

"By this time, her two friends had noticed she was no longer with them and came back out to see what was wrong."

"What about the gun guy?"

"He'd already disappeared."

"That quick?"

"Just blended into the passing crowd, obviously."

"Slick."

Neil nodded. "*Too* damn slick."

"You thinking what I'm thinking?"

"Professional."

"Maybe a hitter, maybe not. Could be some sort of enforcer."

Neil gave me one of his grim expressions. "Yeah. But ya know what we gotta do, right?"

"Exactly. Treat him as a pro."

"And consider ourselves damn lucky if, by some fluke, he turns out to be just some mob shyster."

"Did she give you a description?"

"Six feet, one-fifty, well-dressed, black hair in a buzz cut, dark eyes, low forehead. And carrying a big, scary-ass gun."

"Good description."

Neil nodded. "She's the niece of a damn good cop."

"I'm wondering about the dark eyes and hair. And especially the low forehead. Hispanic, maybe?"

"Might be."

"So now we might be looking at something involving Vega?"

"I'm sure as hell hoping not."

"Did she say anything else?"

"Nope."

"Not even a hint?"

"Nope."

"She didn't by any chance try to follow him, did she? To see where he went? If there was anyone with him?"

"She was so damn scared, she ran into the ladies' room and lost her nut. Once she'd calmed down, she asked them to take her right home. Jane called me about half an hour later, told me about it. This was two days ago."

"You sure she's not into anything else?"

"Positive."

"Then this is all about Grayson. He's the one we have to start looking for."

"No doubt."

Neil got up and began pacing. Pacing, wandering over to the door and scanning the peephole to make sure his cruiser was still parked in the visitor's spot directly across the street next to my TransAm. Then he turned around and checked out my CD and vinyl collection on the shelves of my stereo cabinet. I could tell he was irritated and frustrated and didn't quite know how to handle this. His niece could be involved in something really bad and he didn't want to believe it.

After a few minutes, he came back to the sofa and sat. He didn't say anything and began staring at his hands. I could tell he was really worried and hated asking help from anyone. But he knew he couldn't look into this himself without involving anyone else from the Department and risk it leaking out so everyone knew what was going on. And keeping anything quiet in a building full of cops was impossible.

"So tell me more about this Grayson," I said after a short while.

"I've got some folks trying to find him, but it's hard keeping this low-profile. I wanna question the bastard but I don't want just anyone hearing about it. It this does blow, we'll have to find some place to stash Erin till it dies. That could take weeks, and it could mess up her senior year at Rollins. But if it does involve Vega, I won't want this hanging over her head. Hell, we might have to send her somewhere. Vega's one stubborn Hispanic. And he holds a grudge. He also has one long-ass memory."

"It's obvious someone considers Erin some sort of threat. Or obstacle. Otherwise, she wouldn't have been approached or threatened."

"I talked to her, Deacon. She doesn't know anything."

"How can you know for sure?"

"I talked to the girl for an hour. I used every tactic I knew. Even some of that psychiatric crap they shoved into my skull years ago from a couple of those courses I had to take when I wanted to get promoted. She's a naïve, impressionable young girl. She wasn't hiding anything. I could tell."

"Then we just have to assume that she doesn't know anything, and that someone who's gone to the Goons & Guns store—or owns the Goons & Guns store—thinks she does know something. Or thinks she's standing in someone's way."

"That's about all we can do."

Something had been chafing at my shorts all through this, and I soon found that I couldn't hold it in any longer. "Neil, tell me something."

"Does this have anything to do with why I'm here?"

"Actually, I'm much more interested in why you picked me of all people to help with this."

"Same damn thing, smartass."

"Well, then, let loose with the epiphany."

He sighed. I could tell this was difficult for him. Neil had never been a feelings sort of guy.

"I chose you because this is my sister's daughter, and I can't trust too damn many people at the Station because I've seen too much corruption come into that building in the last fifteen years. I know there are a few honest, really good cops working there, but I have to assume everyone else is corrupt, on the take, not trained well enough or just not trustworthy. I also chose you because you seem to have at least eight senses, and you're never wrong when using them. You've never let me down, and you've never lied to me." He took a long breath. "Now…do we start hugging one another about this time? If that's what you're expecting, don't get your hopes up, because that's where I draw the line."

"No, Neil. I ain't exactly the guy-hugging type, either."

"Thank God for small favors."

Chapter 3

I reached the Police Station at around ten o'clock, just a few minutes before the tail end of the morning rush hour and the additional chaos made by the tour buses had stopped congesting the roads.

Neil was waiting for me in his office. He looked just as irritable as he had in my apartment. He'd pulled down his tie, opened his collar and hiked his shirt sleeves up to his elbows. The effect made him look like someone right out of *Barney Miller*. I could tell this thing with his niece was taking its toll. I couldn't blame him. Neil didn't let himself get too close to people, but he'd always been very protective of his family.

As soon as I walked in, he gave me an instant professional assessment that started at my face and swept right down to my lightweight jacket. Then he looked me right in the eye. "You're carryin', I hope." His quick gaze had assessed the slight bulge beneath my left armpit, where I carried my Cheetah in its tiny chamois holster under my jacket.

I nodded. I didn't normally carry a gun, but sometimes, as in this case, it was necessary. I wasn't afraid of guns, but I wasn't exactly a crack shot, and had never found myself in the situation where I had to actually shoot anyone before. I know how ridiculous that sounded, especially for a top-notch private eye like myself. But when you've got a spirit watching over you giving you valuable tips, it cuts down considerably on surprises—especially when they involve fireworks.

I suspected this was going to be a tough case, and if it involved someone like Arturo Vega, I had to be packing. Vega was the mob boss who'd been controlling Kissimmee the last several years. I'd dealt with the big man before. He used top-notch talent and wasn't someone to be trifled with. He'd ordered one of his psycho gunmen to kidnap me just a few years ago and bring me into his office. But he'd been extremely shrewd about the whole business, and as a result, I'd never even seen the man's face. Even Papa Joc Raguzzo didn't take chances with Vega. And Papa Joe had been controlling Orlando with an iron fist for the last three decades.

"What is it?" Neil asked in a soft voice. "The Bersa? Or the Beretta?"

"I've got the Cheetah. It fits better in my hand."

He nodded. "Good stopper, even if it is only a three-eighty. I just hope you won't need it."

"Me, too."

"Want a backup?" He pointed to his desk. "I've got a .45 hammerless snub-nosed revolver in an Uncle Mike's ankle holster. It's loaded with hollow points, and it's yours if—"

"Thanks. I'm good."

"You're sure?"

I could tell Neil was nervous about all this. Otherwise, he wouldn't have even suggested the backup revolver. Too bad I couldn't tell him about my dead buddy Mike, who'd be helping me with this shortly.

If only she'd show…

It didn't make me feel confident at all that I hadn't seen her in several days. Needless to say, I was beginning to worry if I'd ever see her again.

"Where's your niece?" I figured it was time to get on with this. Mike would appear in her own good time. If I was lucky. "And where exactly do I come in?"

"Right now, she and Benton are still holed up in one of the vacant conference rooms. I asked Benton to keep this one under wraps. If I know her, she's got Erin ready to go."

"Tell me what you want me to do."

Neil blinked. "Keep her safe."

I expected him to go into further detail. He just stood there, staring at me and looking desperate. I'd never seen that expression on him before, and it really hit me. This was a man who was looking at me as if I were his last hope, and I didn't enjoy being placed in that position. But Neil was my friend, and since he'd never been one to ask such a favor, I figured that he had no choice. I also knew that I would not let him down.

"For how long?" I asked.

"Until we find Grayson, figure out what the hell he's into, how Erin's involved, and deliver him to the Feds, if necessary. I'll call and ask you to bring her back to the Station if and when that happens."

"Any idea when that'll be?"

26

Neil suddenly looked frightened. "I wish I knew."

"Then I'm on the clock?"

"As of right now."

I nodded.

He held out his hand. "I'll need your cell."

I knew better than ask questions. If this involved high-powered mob stuff that could work its way back to the Station, my cell could be tracked easily. I pulled it out and handed it to him. He placed it in his top drawer and pulled out another cell. He handed it over.

"Untraceable?"

"The coordinates are jammed, relayed and looped. I've got a friend in on this. He's the only one who's got GPS access. Once the call is scrambled, relayed, looped and whatever else he's got to do, it's sent directly to one of my burner phones. I've got three I'm using for this. Let me know if you have to dump this one. I'll get another one to you really quick."

I pocketed the phone.

"One other thing."

I waited for him to tell me the rest.

"Your TransAm?"

"What about it?"

He didn't speak right off. I could tell something unpleasant was coming. Neil wasn't exactly a die-hard car guy, but he did admire my classic ride. However, his expression told me I wasn't going to appreciate what he was about to say.

27

I decided to make it easier for him. "You don't like my classic ride?"

"That's not it at all."

"Then what's the problem? There is a problem, isn't there? I can tell. You've got that concerned-and-really-irritated expression all over your face."

"As soon as you leave here with Erin, you've got to ditch it."

I opened my mouth to protest. Then realized what he was telling me. "It's that bad?"

He sighed. "I hope not. I really do. But since we don't know what this actually is, who's involved or how high up it goes, we've got to be extra careful."

"I'll need something that moves, you realize. Something I can use to get away from the bad guys without breaking a sweat. And since I won't know what they'll be driving…"

Neil nodded. "Just make sure you get something that's either gray, tan, silver or black. All I see now on the roads is gray, tan, silver or black. The harder we can make it for the assholes involved to snatch her, the better." He dug into his back pocket and pulled out a wad of crisp one-hundred-dollar bills. He peeled off ten and handed them over.

I just stared at them.

"Somethin' wrong?"

"I just didn't expect you to cough up anything without a fight. Especially this much jack."

He pocketed the rest. "She's family, Deacon. Just keep her safe."

28

As I turned to the door, he said, "Ya need more, let me know."

"I'm good. And don't worry. She'll be safe with me."

"I know." For the first time that morning, Neil looked relieved.

As we left his office, I sincerely hoped Mike would turn up soon.

Chapter 4

At around 10:30, Neil and I slipped into one of the conference rooms halfway down the corridor to pick up Erin.

The policewoman sitting beside her was about thirty-five. She was very attractive, with thick black hair and large, long-lashed chestnut eyes. She had a pretty face but did not smile at me even after Neil had introduced us. She stood, reaching my height. She looked fit and trim. I could tell by the way she stood—proud and tall, with her head held high— that Neil's niece was in good hands. This woman was definitely not the type to put up with nonsense. She hardly spoke, nodding at Neil as he told her our itinerary.

Before we left the room, Erin thanked her for her company. The three of us went down the hall, to the rear exit. Just before we went outside, Neil hugged her briefly and whispered, "Do exactly as he says, baby." Erin nodded and whispered back, "I will, Uncle Neil."

Erin and I went outside to the rear parking lot. She was obviously frightened, walking stiffly, her eyes darting everywhere. She hadn't said a word since we'd left the building.

I opened the passenger door of the TransAm, which I'd parked beside one of their police vans. She slid in and I closed the door. She had just one

30

suitcase, as well as a large tan leather handbag. I put both in the back seat and got behind the wheel.

Not wanting to burden her with questions, I didn't say anything. Knowing what it was like to be scared, I decided not to inflict my twisted humor on her. She had enough problems.

I pulled out, crossed the crowded lot and eased out into traffic. In just moments we were engulfed in the heavy downtown flow. Using the mirrors, I carefully monitored the road activity and made constant mental notes of the traffic. Since I'd been in this racket for some time, I considered myself pretty good at spotting red flags. I had fairly good recall when recognizing persistent vehicles — especially after making sudden turns and periodically getting on different roads.

However, tight situations like this made me realize how much I relied on Mike. I sincerely hoped I'd see some sign of her shortly.

After I'd gotten onto Colonial Drive and headed east, Erin asked in a soft voice, "What should I call you?"

"Deacon's fine."

"Is that your first name?"

"No."

She waited. When I didn't reply right off, she said, "What's your first name?"

"Ralph."

"Mind if I call you Ralph?"

"No one else calls me that, but I guess it's okay."

She shifted in her seat and seemed to relax a little. She kept pushing her heavy dark-brown hair away from her face. She was obviously uncomfortable.

"You okay?" I asked.

"I *hate* this wig…" She gave it another shove.

"Take it off, then."

"Uncle Neil told me to keep it on till we find a place to hide."

"Keep it on, then."

She sighed. "But I *hate* it…"

"Take it off, then."

She stared at me in silence for several moments. Then she laughed.

I was relieved that I'd actually lightened the moment. It made me realize that a little levity might make her less tense. "Something funny?"

"Uncle Neil said you were quite a character."

"I didn't think the old boy cared."

"It didn't sound like a compliment when he said it."

I nodded. "Now *that* sounds more like Neil."

"He did say you were the best."

"He didn't."

"He really did."

"No!" I feigned shock.

She laughed. "He also told me that if he found out I told you, he was going to tan my hide."

"I guess we'll just have to keep it our little secret, then."

She nodded and sat back. She went silent again. About half a minute later, she said, "How come you're not asking me anything?"

"Like what?"

She shrugged. "I don't know. Anything, I guess."

"I didn't think you'd want me to."

She just looked at me. I could tell she wanted to say something.

"Are you saying you want me to?"

"I guess so…"

"What would you like me to ask you?"

She stared uneasily at me. I figured she had no idea what I was up to.

I decided to make it a little easier for her. "I take it you're thinking about Grayson?"

She suddenly looked frightened again. Then she turned and glanced out the window.

"I need to get you safe first."

She nodded but didn't say anything.

"Once I switch cars and find a safe place, then you can settle in and take off that stupid wig."

She smiled. It was a nice smile. She was a very pretty girl. "Would you like to know my real hair color?"

"Nope."

"Why not?"

"I like surprises."

"Me, too."

"But only good ones. Believe me, I've had some real bummers."

"I'll bet."

She sounded like she knew what I was talking about.

"You know something about my work?"

She nodded. "I've seen *The Rockford Files*. And *Columbo*. And *Diagnosis Murder*."

I should have known she'd say something like that. I didn't want to make her feel stupid telling her that most TV shows about private eyes were brainless, so I didn't say anything.

"That's why I'm kinda nervous right now," she said, glancing at her side mirror. "I keep expecting a car chase at any minute."

"Don't worry. I'm about to trade in this girl with a different ride."

"Girl?"

"Of course."

She blinked. "You're one of those guys who thinks his car's a *girl*?"

"She really is."

"Why a girl? Why not a guy? This *is* a guy-ride, isn't it?"

I smiled. She'd surprised me again. "You...know cars?"

"I know the ones that fly. This one's hot, right?"

"Blistering, if I let her go."

"But why a girl?"

"She's covered in paint, roars like a lioness, is very demanding, takes me where I wanna go long before I ask her to, and has saved my life many times."

34

Erin thought about that for a moment. "She's like your own very special guardian angel, then."

I thought of Mike again. And missed her all over again. And caught myself glancing at the back seat in the rearview.

The empty back seat...

"I wish," I said softly.

"What was that?"

"Just thinking aloud."

"You look so...sad..."

"I just don't like trading in my girl," I lied. And thought of Mike again.

"I understand."

She really didn't, but I nodded anyway.

***

We stopped at a car rental place on Semoran Boulevard shortly after eleven.

Since I'd dealt with the same place several times before, they remembered me. They also let me park the TransAm in the back of the building, out of sight from the busy highway.

I selected a shiny tan Charger with not too many miles on it. I wanted a Charger because I'd read about the model and heard from several sources that the car was easy to handle and maneuver, and flew like a scalded cat. Erin stayed in the TransAm while I went inside the small, one-story concrete building and handled the transaction.

Once finished, I went out back, where the TransAm was parked about twenty feet from the rear entrance, between a dark-blue utility van and a maroon Ford pickup. Erin kept close beside me as

35

we entered the crowded side lot and found the Charger. I put her suitcase in the back seat, held the door open for her as she got in, then got behind the wheel.

I was pleased that the side windows had the darkest tint allowable by Florida law. I'd mentioned my preference to Jim, manager of the place, but didn't expect them to comply. I didn't expect anyone to comply to the consumer nowadays and considered it a rare treat when someone actually did.

As I checked out the controls and the fancy options on the dash, Erin said, "It's dark in here."

"That's exactly what I wanted."

She went silent for a moment. Then she said, "I gotcha. Harder to see us, right?"

"One thing you'll eventually learn about me is that although I might seem stupid, dense and distracted most of the time, I'm really not. A few people I've dealt with over the years even think I know what I'm doing."

"I never thought you were stupid…"

"Just dense and distracted?"

"Neither."

I grinned. "Girl, you and I are gonna get along great."

"Not *too* great, I'm hoping." Mike suddenly materialized in the back seat directly behind me. Her beautiful face was hazy but stern. "It's taken me years to teach you to do things that won't get you killed. Don't ruin all my hard work by falling

36

for a pretty face young enough to be your daughter."

Chapter 5

"Why are you grinning like that?" Erin asked as I pulled onto Semoran Boulevard and headed north.

I glanced at Mike's hazy reflection in the rearview and tried hard not to be obvious. It was difficult. I hadn't seen nor heard from Mike in several days and was worried that I'd never see her again. I'd read things about spirits passing over and feared that Mike's spirit might have left me for good. After all, she'd been appearing to me fairly regularly for the last several years. It wasn't like her to let so much time pass without stopping by, even if the visit turned out to be a brief one.

"Ralph?" Erin looked worried. A thick long strand of her brown wig dangled over her left eye. She ignored it completely. "You okay?"

I glanced at Mike once again—just to make sure she was still there. She hadn't vanished, and for the first time since Neil had come to visit me, I knew things might actually turn out okay. "I'm just fine now."

"Now?"

"As opposed to before."

"Did I miss something?" Confusion covered her face.

"Not really. I'm good. Honestly."

"Well, you had me scared. In fact, you still do."

"How so?"

"Just a minute ago, you were grinning like you'd just won the Lottery or something. And when I asked you why, you got this weird expression on your face. And when I asked if you were okay, you just sighed and seemed happy again. Is there something you wanna tell me? Or is this something that doesn't concern me?"

"This is going to be interesting," Mike said with a wry grin.

"I've suddenly got this feeling that everything will turn out just fine."

"Really?"

"Yep."

"You mean, like kismet?"

"Something like that."

"I take it you missed me," Mike said, still smiling.

"A lot."

"Pardon?" Erin asked.

"Everything's gonna turn out just fine. A lot."

"Okay…" Erin turned to face the windshield, but I could still see the confusion on her face.

"I can't wait to find out what this is all about," Mike said, smiling.

I wanted to tell her but decided against it for obvious reasons.

I'd already frightened Erin enough for one afternoon.

***

I drove a few miles north on Semoran, turned onto Aloma and worked my way west, onto Osceola, taking it until I turned onto Lee Road.

My plan was to drive to South Orange Blossom Trail and find a motel. The Trail was my first choice since the strip clubs and its plethora of businesses and strip malls made it a hectic stretch of highway. Due to the chaos, it would provide us anonymity. It would be much more difficult to spot a silver Charger in extremely heavy traffic, and even more difficult to keep tabs on it amongst such chaotic activity. And since it was rapidly approaching lunchtime, the traffic situation would be even more abysmal.

As I'd suspected, traffic stayed congested on Lee Road. This was a good thing, especially since I hadn't noticed anything suspicious. Just a short time later, I made a left onto the Trail and took it several miles south, until I felt reasonably safe that we hadn't caught a tail. Traffic had become worse, the endless intersections and four-way lights turning the stretch into a sea of blinding metal and glass. I continued using both my side and rearview mirrors, scanning the throngs clogging all possible lanes.

As always, Mike automatically took my lead and watched as well, making my job less stressful. With Mike, I didn't have to tell her much. She knew me well enough to figure out what was going on very quickly.

I'd wanted to drive a few miles farther south but decided this area our best bet for right now. It wasn't the best section in town, but its constant state of chaos would make the situation more difficult for the people after Erin to know where we were.

A couple of miles farther south, I stopped at a Motor Inn. I pulled up to the front entrance and parked on the other side of a BMW in the front lot to hide the Charger from the busy highway.

"Here?" Erin suddenly looked frightened. She nudged closer to the door.

I glanced at the entrance. No one was walking toward us or approaching the Charger from the rear. "What's wrong? The place is fairly acceptable for this area. It looks clean, judging by the fact that I see no trash lying around. There are a bunch of cars in the lot, and almost all of them have out-of-state tags. It stands to reason that if the tourists are staying here, it can't be so bad."

She didn't reply. Just kept looking scared.

"Do you want me to look for another place?"

After a short silence, she said in a soft voice, "No…"

"Then what's the problem?"

"I think she might be afraid of you," Mike said.

I glanced at her hazy reflection in the rearview.

Mike shrugged. "A middle-aged man? A young, impressionable, vulnerable girl? Do the math."

I still didn't know what she was getting at.

Mike, as usual, sensed my cluelessness. She sighed. "The sex thing, silly."

"Oh…" It finally registered, and I felt like an idiot. I turned to Erin. "Listen. I know you're young and pretty and all, and probably have all these wild ideas and misconceptions about guys my age, especially when we're alone with young girls like you… But let me put it to you this way. You've got nothing to worry about. Nothing at all."

She didn't say anything right off. She was studying my face, possibly to determine if I was telling her the truth. Then she nodded. "I getcha."

"Good." Then I discovered that the expression on her face wasn't the one I was looking for. "Do you really?"

She shrugged. "You're gay."

Mike laughed.

I held back a groan. It amazed me how so many females thought that just because a man wasn't interested, he had to be gay. It was undoubtedly their way of justifying the rejection issue without feeling inferior. "I'm not gay."

"Really?"

"Really."

She looked confused. "Then, if you're not gay, why don't you want to—"

"To repeat myself, I'm not gay. I love women. All sorts of women. I've loved babes all my life. In fact, I prefer them to men, and would die with a huge smile on my face if I had to deal with them exclusively for the rest of my days. They're infinitely better-looking, softer, easier on the eyes, smell better, and are much smarter and ten times more interesting."

"My…" Mike blinked. "That sure was a mouthful."

"Okay…" Smiling, Erin seemed to appreciate my testimonial. Then, after a moment or two, she

42

began to frown. "Then why aren't you attracted to me?"

I felt like laughing in spite of the fact that I was getting irritated.

She blinked. "You're not...are you?" She seemed worried again. I had an idea what was coming. A moment later, she proved me right. "Is there something wrong with...I mean, is there something about me that you don't—"

"Girl, don't even go there."

"But there must be *some* reason why you don't wanna—"

"You're Neil's niece."

Her worried look vanished completely and was quickly replaced by total cluelessness.

"Neil's my friend."

She sighed. "But—"

"My friend," I repeated.

"But what does that have to do with—"

"There's an unwritten law between friends."

"You mean—"

"To put it simply, there's a line a true friend will not cross. Making a pass with his wife, ex-wife, girlfriend, daughter or niece definitely defines this line."

She thought about that, then nodded. "I think I get it."

"Good."

"I wondered, but now that I know, it's pretty obvious."

"Obvious how?"

"I can tell you like girls."

43

"I don't like girls. As I just said, I *love* girls."

Erin smiled.

"I mean it."

"I can tell."

"In other words, if you weren't Neil's niece...and if I was twenty years younger...and if this wasn't an actual *job*...and if there weren't bad guys out there, looking for you..." I shrugged. "Get it now?"

Still smiling, she nodded.

"Now that we've finally cleared up my sexual preferences, philosophies and motivations...can I go inside now and get us a room?"

She didn't reply.

"And just in case you're wondering about the sleeping accommodations, I'll be happy to take the couch."

She smiled.

"I guess your smile—as well as the fact that you no longer look like you're ready to toss your breakfast—means it's okay for me to get us a room now?"

Erin nodded.

"Great. Now lock the doors and stay in the car, okay?"

"I will."

I opened my door. "One last thing."

"Yes?"

"You can unlock the door for me when I come back. Think you can remember that?"

She laughed.

44

Chapter 6

Mike appeared right beside me as I was paying for the room.

She didn't say anything—which suited me fine. I wasn't exactly in the mood to explain our bizarre relationship to anyone—especially a bored, disinterested motel clerk. I just leaned against the counter and watched as he handled the paperwork and inserted my card into the reader.

Once he gave me my receipt and returned my card, I went back outside. Mike stayed beside me. I stepped off the sidewalk and crossed the paved front lot that would take us back to the Charger.

Mike decided right then that it was time to start asking questions.

"So, from I've already gathered, you're keeping that young girl safe?"

"That's about it."

"What exactly is going on?"

"She might have been involved with the wrong guy."

"Wrong guy? As in bad boy? Or criminal?"

"Probably both."

"She's kind of young for that, right?"

"You know about impressionable girls, don't you? Weren't you one of those when you were alive?"

"Strangely, I was never into the bad boy scene. I usually preferred my guys to have more than two or three I. Q. points."

"I stand corrected."

"Anyway, this is why you're here, getting a room? Are why you're on a case? And why she was afraid you'd be a pervert?"

"By the way, where the hell have you been?" It seemed to be the most important thing on my mind, and I knew I wouldn't be able to concentrate on anything else until she told me what was going on. I moved over to a parked SUV so Erin wouldn't see me standing out there in front of the building, talking to myself.

"Pardon me?"

"I've been going out of my mind." I turned around to make sure the motel guy wasn't watching. He'd apparently left his post and disappeared in his office. Possibly to take a leak or grab a sandwich. "I was afraid you'd passed over. And that I'd never see you again. I was also afraid that when I *did* see you again, it would be only for a moment. And you wouldn't be able to spend any time with me anymore. And—"

"You did miss me, didn't you?" Mike was smiling.

Her smile usually made me feel terrific. But not now. I was much too upset. I realized only then that I was more pissed off and frustrated than usual. "You could say that, yeah."

"So tell me, what's happening here? Who is she? Someone I need to worry about?"

46

"Mike, why won't you tell me what's going on?"

She gave me one of her clueless looks. Needless to say, it didn't do anything for me right now. "Going *on*?"

"You know. Staying away. Not showing up. Avoiding me. Making me think you'd crossed over. That sort of thing."

"I did cross over."

I nearly gasped. Was she serious? She looked serious. I couldn't see any evidence of her usual playfulness in her large, beautiful almond eyes. But how could she cross over and still come back here?

"If you crossed over, then how are you here?"

"I crossed over a long time ago, silly."

"Really?"

"Yes."

"Then how are you still able to—"

"I can't explain things to you as they are, but basically, it's like this. When a spirit is connected to a mortal, the spirit sticks around as long as he or she is needed."

"But I always need you."

"Which is why I keep coming back and helping you, silly."

"But why has it been so long since—"

"Since you've seen me?"

"Let's go with that, yeah."

"Time is different with us. We don't have that annoying twenty-four-hour window thingy to worry about. Not in the spirit world, that is."

"You mean—"

47

"What I mean is, I might have been gone for three days in your world, but for me, it was just a few moments."

"But when you're here—"

"When I'm here, time drags. It's that way because I'm stuck in that irritating time frame. The rotation of the earth, the irritating clock thing, the whole nine yards. Didn't I tell you all this a long time ago?"

I shrugged. "Probably."

"You obviously forgot."

As usual, she made me feel guilty. And also stupid. "A lot on my mind, I guess."

She shook her head. "You really are silly, you know."

"Tell me something I don't know."

"*Touché*. So then…tell me more about this case."

I told her all about it as we crossed the lot and approached the Charger. When I'd finished, she said, "Is this why you're not driving your lady?"

"Neil told me to switch it with something else. Something less conspicuous."

"That makes sense. She does stick out quite a bit, you know."

"I know."

"You've made several enemies over the years. I'm sure they're all familiar with that car."

I nodded.

She smiled. "This new number is sleek. Nice-looking, too."

"I guess so..." I began feeling more nostalgic than usual.

"You miss her, don'tcha?"

I nodded. "I'm miserable about it, too."

"Where'd you leave her? At the car rental?"

"Yeah. And she'd better be there when I'm finished with this job."

"How are you going to keep in touch with your rude police friend?"

"He gave me a burner phone."

"And this is simply a job where you keep close to her to make sure she's not harmed or kidnapped?"

"Basically."

"And how long will this take?"

"As long as it takes."

"That narrows it down."

"I'm just glad you're here. I really need an extra set of eyes."

"That makes me feel *so* wanted."

"Believe me, you are."

Mike smiled. "I know. You've already stated that several times in the last five minutes."

"Sorry. I guess I was just overwhelmed."

"Well, I'm here now, so you can relax."

"Right. I'm holed up with a pretty twenty-year-old female in a motel room, and no doubt facing men from Vega's organization looking for us so they can grab her and kill me if I get in their way. I'm really and truly totally relaxed."

"You have me, now, don't you?"

"That's the one thing in my favor."

"Then stop acting silly and try to relax."

"You actually think I can do both?"

"A girl can always hope..."

Chapter 7

Erin waited in the Charger while Mike and I went inside the motel room to check things out.

Since Erin was so nervous and obviously had never been through something like this before, I'd ordered a double room and hoped she'd be more relaxed with a little privacy. Judging by what Neil had said about her, she had no prior experience with criminals or any sort of illegal activity, making this very frightening and difficult for her to handle. Anything I could do to make this more tolerable for her would be a plus.

Once I'd inspected the rooms, I went back outside and pulled out her suitcase from the back seat of the Charger. She took it as I grabbed my overnight case. Then I followed her inside and locked the door while Erin stood in the center of the room, looking at everything.

"Your room's on the other side of that door," I told her.

"*Two* rooms? Totally cool!" Taking her suitcase and handbag, she hurried into the next room and switched on the light. "This isn't so bad at all..." I heard her drop the suitcase onto the bed and click it open.

"What should we be waiting for?" Mike asked.

I put my overnight case on the dresser beside the TV. "Nothing, I hope," I whispered. "Otherwise, we'll have to move to a different motel."

"What exactly is your rude police buddy doing about all this?"

I took out my cell and held it close to my face—just in case Erin came back out and asked who I was talking to. "He's got a couple of trusted people involved. Erin's his niece, so this is personal. He knows he can't trust many people in the Department, and it's hitting him hard."

"No doubt." Mike glanced at the phone in my hand. "Who're you calling?"

"No one."

"Then why are you—"

"This is just in case she hears me whispering and wants to know—"

"Ralph?" Erin came out of the room and gazed at me as I stood in front of the mirror, holding the phone.

"I'm still here."

She gawked at my cell. "Who're you talking to?"

I sighed. This wasn't the first time I realized that dealing with two women at the same time was going to be the death of me. "No one."

"Then why are you holding—"

"I wanted to check to see if the batteries were low. What did you want?"

"Did I hear you whispering?"

52

I shrugged. "I was cussing because I couldn't get the damned thing to respond, and I didn't want you to hear me."

She smiled. "Okay... so what do we do about food?"

"Food?"

She shrugged. "You know. That stuff you eat? Put in your stomach? Digest it if you're lucky?"

Mike laughed.

"I know what food is," I said flatly.

Erin frowned. "For a moment, I wondered. It seems to be the last thing on your mind."

"Possibly because your safety is the *first* thing on my mind. Priorities, as they say."

"I appreciate that, I really do. So then, all you're doing right now is checking the batteries in your phone?"

"I do that a lot."

"Seriously?"

"In my line of work, you need to keep a constant eye on those pesky cell phone batteries."

"Clever," Mike said.

"I never thought of that," Erin said.

"You would if you were a private eye. And needed your cell phone to work if you found yourself caught in a firefight and needed backup in a hurry. Or just got shot and had to call nine-one-one before you went unconscious."

"You're making me feel, well, kind of stupid right now," she said.

"How could you know about this stuff unless you did this for a living?"

53

"I guess I really should know about it."

"Why?"

"My uncle's a cop."

"How often do you see him?"

"Not very. Maybe two, three times a month."

"Then it's all right to feel stupid about this."

Erin studied my expression to determine if I was kidding. "I guess so…"

"Is that all you wanted? To ask about food?"

She nodded. "I really am hungry. Except for a cup of coffee and some toast this morning, I haven't eaten all day. I just wondered if you had any idea what we could do about dinner—"

"We passed a boatload of places on our way here, if you remember."

"I remember."

"Then there should be no problem, right?"

"I guess not…" Her brow crinkled.

"That sounded like a problem. Is there a problem?"

She nodded.

"What's the problem?"

She shrugged. "I'm really hungry."

***

Five minutes later, Mike and I headed down the Trail, looking for a place to buy supper.

Before we left, Erin told me she liked seafood and charbroiled steak. She especially loved pizza and could eat it every day of the week. But she couldn't eat Mexican at all, and actually preferred fried chicken or shrimp if she couldn't get pizza.

"I guess tonight will be pizza night," Mike said as we pulled up to the front entrance of a Papa John's.

"What gave it away?" I asked.

Mike pointed to the building facing us. "For a start, I'd say the huge color pictures of pizzas slapped all over the front windows. Not to mention the word "pizza" on the sign right off the entrance. And the other signs saying "pizza" as well as the collage of different pizza combos covering the front door."

"Gotta keep her happy," I told her as I parked the Charger and got out. "She's going through a shitload of stress. Comfort food, as they say."

"Not to mention the fact that you love pizza as well, right?"

I grinned. "As we Italians have been saying for hundreds of years, pizza is God's most perfect food."

Mike just shook her head.

Chapter 8

Rush hour turned out to be as bad as I'd expected. It took me more than twenty minutes to cover the two-mile stretch from the pizza place back to the motel.

Mike and I got back a little after four-thirty. However, I quickly realized that traffic was going to be the least of my worries the moment I pulled into the motel entrance and eased the Charger up to the parking place facing the room.

A tall, broad-shouldered man talked on a cell a few doors down. His back was turned. He didn't flinch or glance in my direction as I pulled up and parked less than twenty feet from where he was. This made me wary. Most people, in similar circumstances, would instinctively turn upon hearing an engine getting closer. Or turn, see what was making the noise, then move a fair distance away so they could continue their phone conversation.

Since I was working on something that could most likely turn dangerous, I was automatically on edge, and sensitive to anything even slightly suspicious. And in my experience, when someone didn't turn in the direction of an approaching vehicle, they seemed highly suspect.

"Trouble?" Mike asked.

"I'm not sure."

"When do you think you'll be sure?"

"When I open the car door, get out, and walk up to the motel room."

"And…?"

"I'll be able to tell by that guy's reaction if he's someone I should worry about."

"What reaction are you hoping for?"

"I'm really hopeful that he'll just keep standing there, talking on his cell."

"What if he doesn't?"

I reached under my jacket and took the clasp off my Cheetah. "Then I'll probably have to use this."

"Are you forgetting me?" she asked.

"How can I possibly do that? It took you forever to get back into my life. How can I ignore you?"

She scowled. "You're not gonna forgive me for that, are you?"

"It's something I wasn't ready for at the time."

"Let me help you get through this, okay?"

"Any ideas?"

"You really don't have to ask me that, do you?"

"Just surprise me, then."

She smiled. "That I can do."

I pushed open the door, got out and took the two boxes of pizza over to the motel room door. My left hand held the swipe card. My right rested underneath the pizza boxes, my hand tightly gripping the butt of the Cheetah .380.

57

I watched the man as I reached the door. He didn't turn or even glance in my direction. He just kept talking into his cell.

Mike's hazy form drifted over in his direction.

Relieved that she was with me again, I went inside and locked the door behind me.

***

Erin was sitting on the couch, watching something on the TV. The moment she saw me, she sat bolt upright. "What's wrong?"

"Why do you ask?" I turned away slightly to holster the Cheetah so she wouldn't see me doing it.

"You look worried. Something happen?"

I shrugged and forced myself to smile. I didn't want to do or say anything to alarm her, especially since it had taken so much effort earlier to make her believe that I wasn't going to jump her bones the moment we came inside the room. "Too much damned traffic." I handed her one of the boxes and put the second one on the table in the corner, behind the door.

"Thank you *so* much!" Apparently, all it took was fresh hot pizza to get her back on track. She opened the box, carefully pulled out a triangular piece and eased a small wedge of it into her mouth. Bits of tomato sauce gathered at the corners of her mouth and just above her chin.

"Want a towel?" I asked.

She laughed and covered her mouth. Her cheeks reddened. She coughed, and I had visions of performing the Heimlich Maneuver while waiting for the paramedics to arrive. Recovering, she

58

grabbed one of the napkins from the bag I'd brought and blotted her face. Once she'd swallowed that first mouthful, she snatched up her iced tea to help it down. Taking a deep breath, she sat back. Her cheeks were still red. "I'm sorry. I know I'm embarrassing sometimes, but I really can't help it." She shrugged. "I mean, this is *pizza!*"

"You're singing to the choir, babe." I pulled a piece loose from my box, sat down on the couch beside her and started eating. Something quickly made the back of my neck tingle as I watched Erin push another small portion of the delicious food into her mouth. Something wrong. Something that shouldn't have happened. Something that definitely didn't fit in with this scenario.

I couldn't quite put my finger on it out until she grabbed the can and had another slug. Then it dawned on me, and my defenses instantly went up. "Where'd you get that?"

She blinked. "Huh?"

"That iced tea. You didn't have it when I left."

She smiled. "You really *are* a detective, aren'tcha?"

"That's what my tax returns say in the occupation box. And what the stencils on my office door spell out."

"You really are funny, you know." She was smiling as she nibbled on another piece of her slice.

"I've been told that once or twice before." She was beginning to irritate me. Since she was related to a cop I knew well and admired, I'd been hopeful that she'd turn out to be a cut or two above the other

59

females her age. But right now, I was thinking horrible thoughts, and reminded myself to cool it. "So please answer my original question."

"You mean about the iced tea?"

"There's a good start. Let's try that and see where it goes."

She raised her left hand and jabbed a thumb at the wall behind her. "The machines are down the breezeway, on our left. Between the buildings."

My pulse raced. I nearly jumped up. "You...left the room?"

"Just for a minute. I was thirsty."

I still didn't believe what she'd done. "You actually left the room? While I was gone?"

She just stared at me. She wasn't getting it.

"I specifically told you to stay here."

"I know, but like I said—"

"You know what this is all about, don't you? That thing with Grayson? The guy with the gun approaching you? The guy with the gun wanting you to come with him? The guy with the gun disappearing the moment your buds showed up?"

Her cheeks had suddenly paled. "Well, yeah, but—"

"These people aren't playing around. They mean business. And since they're looking for you, they're gonna find you. One way or the other. Believe me. They're good. Real good."

"I was just gone for two minutes..." Her voice had become a whisper.

"These people can do a lot of damage in two minutes."

"You're *scaring* me…"

"I need to. You obviously aren't assessing the situation, so…" I held out my hands. "I guess I really *need* to slap a giant scare into you."

Mike appeared a couple of feet on my left. Her expression was grim. "We need to talk."

"I'm sorry," Erin said, "but if I knew that getting a can of iced tea would bother you so much—"

"Now," Mike said.

"We'll continue this later. I've got to use the bathroom."

"But—"

"Do me a large favor, all right? I mean, a *very* large favor? Actually, a ginormous one. In fact, promise me you'd rather die than *not* do this very large, ginormous favor for me."

"W-What's that?" she asked tensely.

"Whatever you do, do *not* raise that butt of yours off that couch while I'm gone."

Chapter 9

I closed the bathroom door behind me.

Mike was already standing in front of the shower stall, that same grim expression covering her hazy face. This frightened me because I knew her very well and knew that when she looked this way, something bad had just happened. Or would soon happen.

"What's up?" I whispered.

"I think whoever you're hiding her from has found out she's here."

I felt a tingle of ice shimmer down my spine. "Are you sure?"

"Yes."

"How?"

"I'm not certain. I just know."

"What happened with the guy talking on the cell?"

"The moment you came inside with the pizza, he slipped between the buildings and ran down the walk, to the other side of the complex. He was still talking on his cell when he got behind the wheel of a black Lexus."

"Did you find out who he was talking to?"

"It was another man."

"Did you hear much?"

"Enough."

"Any names?"

"No names."

"What about their conversation?"

"The man he was talking to told him to keep an eye on the Charger. He said he'd send three men and they'd be there in about half an hour."

My first question was how anyone had found out about the Charger so quickly. But I knew I didn't have the luxury of thinking that out right now. "Damn. That doesn't give us much time."

"No. It doesn't."

"Did you find out anything else about who the guy in the Lexus was talking to?"

"He sounded Hispanic, but the conversation was in English. This suggests—at least, to me—that the other guy probably doesn't speak Spanish. They both mentioned Erin, and the guy on the other end said they had to find some way to get her away from you."

"They say why?"

Mike shook her head.

"Half an hour?"

"Less than that now."

"I've got to get her out of here."

"Without that guy seeing you do it. He was given strict instructions to stay close."

"That's the tricky part. I've got to somehow disable that Lexus if I want to make it back to the motel room and get Erin away. But I've got to do it quickly."

"I know."

"Any ideas?"

"I might have some way of distracting him. How long will it take you to disable his car?"

"Two minutes, tops."

"What are you gonna do?"

"Flatten the tires. It's the fastest way of crippling a vehicle. I can't risk trying to get inside and popping the lid. Those high-quality rides have all sorts of anti-tampering devices. Flattening the tires will probably activate the alarm system, but I'm kind of out of options right now."

"You're not gonna shoot him, are you?"

"Too noisy. I don't want a shitload of tourists wandering around out there, making things worse. I brought along a sharp penknife. All I need is for you to distract him for a couple of minutes. After I flatten the tires, I'll work my way back and get Erin back in the car."

"How long for that?"

"No more than five minutes."

"I'll see what I can do."

She disappeared before I could reply.

***

Erin was still sitting on the couch, finishing her slice of pizza when I went back out into the main room.

She'd turned my way the moment she saw me. Her eyes grew enormous. She could obviously see the alarm on my face.

"We've got to get out of here." I tried sounding as calm as possible, but judging by her expression, I hadn't done a very good job of it.

"Are you saying—"

64

"Now."

She searched my face, looking for clues. For anything that would help her understand what was going on. "What happened? I mean, just a moment ago—"

"We've been found."

"Found?"

"Good. You're paying attention. Found. Discovered. Located. Tracked. Get it?"

"But—"

"No buts." There wasn't time for this. I was barely holding myself together. I just hoped she wouldn't come apart on me. I couldn't very well explain to Neil why I'd been forced to deck his niece because she lost it and went hysterical at the wrong time. "Listen to me and do exactly as I say. Understand?"

She nodded.

"Box up the rest of that pizza and go get your things. I'll be at the front door. When I give you the signal, you bring everything and follow me outside. I'll load up the car and we're out of here. Got it?"

"But—"

"I *said*, got it?" Her clueless expression was really doing a job on my nerves. I was aware that in normal situations, she was undoubtedly extremely smart. But right now, she was acting as if she hadn't the vaguest notion where she could hunt down the nearest available brain cell.

She took a breath. "I *think* so…"

"I don't need you to think. Not right now, anyway. I need you to do exactly as I say. You can think later, if we can get out of this in one piece."

My last statement had obviously frightened her. She'd turned pale and began trembling.

I knew I'd gone a little too far, but I had to let her know the situation in a hurry. "Let me put it to you another way. If you want to be kidnapped and bundled up or knocked unconscious by a bunch of bad guys who are not going to be nice, gentle, or the least bit polite, just sit there and finish your pizza. I'll leave and you won't have to ask me any more stupid questions. But if you want to live, shut up and do exactly what I just said."

Without another word she slammed the pizza box shut, jumped up from the couch, spun around and hurried into the next room.

***

No one was standing near the Lexus or sitting in it.

As soon as I approached it, Mike materialized on my left. "You've got about a minute."

"What did you do?"

"He's down at the end of the building, checking the bushes."

"Why would he be checking the bushes?"

"He might've heard something strange coming from them, and went to investigate."

I knew better than question her. I went over to the Lexus. Using my knife, I slit both tires on the driver's side. The moment I penetrated the rubber on the side of the front tire, the alarm went off.

"Dammit. I was right."

"I guess you were."

I turned and spotted someone running in our direction from the other side of the parking lot. "No time to pat myself on the back. We need to split."

I darted between the buildings, making my way back to the motel room.

Chapter 10

Erin, Mike, and I were back on the road within the next few minutes.

I stayed quiet for the first couple of miles. I was nervous and confused and trying to figure out why things had gone wrong so quickly. And, of course, I was still out of breath from my mad dash back to the motel room. I was in pretty good shape, but the spontaneous sprint had winded me. At over forty, your body just doesn't perform nearly as well as you need it to. Especially in emergencies.

I kept glancing at Erin, who sat beside me, staring straight ahead, her eyes as big as silver dollars. Despite her anxious state, I had to find out what happened and how the opposition had found us so quickly. I didn't want to suspect Erin, but there didn't seem to be any other way this could have happened. I needed to find out what was going on before anyone else found us. I was still concerned about the iced tea incident, but I knew I had to give her the benefit of the doubt before accusing her of anything.

However, I understood how this would play out if I didn't handle it just right. As with nearly all young, impressionable girls, Erin was sensitive. Defensive. Easily hurt. I had to be gentle, but I also had to work on this as quickly as possible. In my professional opinion, it just seemed that there was no logical way anyone could have found us unless it had happened from her end.

"Any idea what's going on?" I asked.

She didn't reply. She didn't hear me or had zoned out completely.

"You still with me?"

She turned in my direction and glared. "Why should *I* have any idea what's going on?" She sounded a little too defensive to suit me.

"Because I'm a professional, and I've done everything by the book in this case."

"You're not accusing *me* of anything, are you?" she asked after a slight pause.

"I'm just trying to figure out what the hell's going on."

"Are you saying that just because you don't know what's going on, it's got to be *my* fault?"

"Actually, I don't remember saying that at all."

"Then just what *are* you saying?"

"Just this. I have no idea how the opposition found us, but they did."

"How do you know?"

"How do I know what?"

"How do you know anyone found us?"

I wondered if she was kidding. If she was, it didn't show. But no one could ignore what had happened. No one, that is, who didn't know what was going on. "You're kidding, aren't you?"

"I'm dead serious. Did you actually see anyone out there?"

"There was a guy standing a few doors down when I got back from my pizza run."

"How do you know?"

"How do I know what?"

"How do you know that the guy you saw was a bad guy?"

"I know what I'm doing. I can tell when someone—"

"How do you know that whoever you saw wasn't just a guest? It *was* a motel, after all…"

"Believe me. I know."

"But how?"

"As I just said, I'm a professional."

"And that automatically enables you to tell who's suspicious and who's not just a regular guest? For all we know, the man could have been wandering around, maybe looking for the cold drink machines."

"I have a keen nose for these things."

"But you're not sure…"

"She's got a point," Mike said behind me.

I ignored her. This was not the time to doubt myself. "I'm pretty damned sure."

"How?"

"Listen to me. I'm the boss here, okay?"

She obviously didn't like that. "If you're gonna throw *that* in my face every time I ask you a question—"

"I'm just trying to remind you why I'm here. And why I'm driving you around. And why I rented a car. And two adjoining motel rooms. And why I'm driving around right now, looking for another motel room to toss good money at."

"None of this tells me why you're so certain that there was actually a bad guy standing outside our room."

"She's got another point," Mike said. "I kinda think you'd better try a different tactic here."

"You're right," I told Mike.

"You *agree* with me?" Erin said.

"I'm gonna put this to you bluntly, and I would really like a straight answer."

"I thought you were already being blunt."

"You didn't by any chance *call* anyone while I was out on that pizza run, did you?"

She went silent.

"Looks like you just hit a nerve," Mike said.

"Well? Did you?"

She still didn't reply.

"Is that a yes? Or a no?"

No reply. I knew right then that I needed to shock her with some cold reality.

Without warning, I veered off the main road, turned into a shopping center and eased down the main drag. I took the Charger down the alley between the supermarket and an independent shoe store, coaxing the car farther down, past half a dozen dumpsters, a junk car, and a Goodwill collection box.

I parked facing a slender strip of pine trees running parallel to the rear lot. Then I flicked off the ignition and turned to face her. "Before we do anything else, I'd like you to answer my last question."

Obviously frightened, Erin kept gawking at the trees just twenty feet or so directly beyond the windshield. She seemed afraid that I might drop her off and run. After a few deep breaths, she turned back to me. "Which question was that?"

"The one where I asked you if you called anyone while I was out, getting your pizza."

She looked down.

"Another nerve," Mike said.

"Well?"

She pushed her hands through her hair and sighed.

"Girl, let me put this to you another way. You're in serious trouble. And since your uncle is paying me to watch over you and keep you safe, I'm in serious trouble, too. Some extremely bad guys are anxious to hook up with you, and you know damned well it's not for a romantic evening drinking wine and reading poetry under a starry sky. They think you have something they want."

"I don't."

"Or they think you might know something you're not supposed to know."

"I'd only seen Johnny Grayson a couple of times. They were just casual dates. He didn't tell me anything—"

"Whatever it is, these people consider it important. They'll grab you and put you somewhere isolated so they can take their time finding out what you know or don't know. They think you're some sort of threat, and these boys deal harshly with threats. In other words, when they find us, they're not going to be very nice. They're going to kill me if I get in the way—which I will be, because it's my job. And once I'm out of the picture, they'll keep you with them as long as they have to, until they find out what they're looking for. And when they're finished with you—"

"Stop. Please *stop*."

"I'm just telling you—"

"You're *scaring* me!"

"Erin…"

She was no longer listening. She'd bent forward and buried her face in her hands.

While she sat hunched over in the seat, crying quietly, I leaned back and tried to imagine what was going on. Why she'd reacted so defensively to my questions. I didn't want to suspect her of doing anything stupid, but I had to force myself to look at this logically. Erin was a twenty-year-old girl—which, in itself, made her a liability. I never liked sticking people into categories. I'd always made it a practice to consider them as individuals. But I had to face facts. Erin was intelligent, athletic, personable, and in many ways, mature for her age. But she was still a young girl, and subject to all the trappings and shortcomings of this particular group.

This made her highly suspect.

It also made me wonder what she'd done that had caused our cover to be blown. I was still considering the iced tea incident but knew that what happened had to be more than just that. I'd been gone nearly an hour on that pizza run. That gave her ample time to contact whoever she wanted.

73

There were three crucial questions I had to consider. The first one, of course, was this: who the hell had she contacted? The second was: how had she done it? And the third, and most important: why would she even consider contacting anyone?

After about five minutes, I handed her some Kleenex and decided to give her a few more minutes. Once she'd collected herself, I'd ask her more questions. If she was hiding something, she wouldn't voluntarily tell me anything she didn't want me to know. But since I knew how to ask certain questions to get to the truth, I might find out exactly how everything had gone down the tubes.

I glanced at the rearview mirror.

Mike was no longer in the back seat.

I was just about to panic when she reappeared. As before, her expression was grim. "We just ran out of time," she said.

Without speaking, I gave her my standard look of total blankness.

"There's a dark sedan out there, snooping around."

I didn't want to jump the gun and go apeshit. I just shrugged and hoped Mike would tell me the rest quickly.

"There are three tough-looking guys in it, and they're all armed."

"Oh, good."

Erin sniffed and wiped the tears from her eyes and wet cheeks. "What did you say?"

"Stay here." I reached underneath my seat and grabbed the tape-covered metal sap I used for

74

emergencies. It was a hard metal slug, about the size of my thumb, attached to a six-inch chain. The other end of the chain was screwed to a leather handle I had custom-made a few years ago. It delivered hell of a blow and enabled me to sucker and disarm an armed man without getting involved in an actual struggle. In this case, I was facing three armed men. I needed whatever advantage I could dream up.

"W-What's *that*?" she whispered nervously.

"Just stay here. And don't do anything."

She must have seen the alarm in my eyes. She froze in her seat.

I eased open the door, slipped out into the growing darkness and gently pushed the door closed until it quietly caught the latch. Then I crossed the alley and made my way toward the end of the building, where a Goodwill drop-off box, crammed with old clothes and sheets, sat unattended.

Mike drifted over.

"What's going on?" I whispered.

"One of them was dropped off and is coming here. He's about ten feet away, moving very quietly."

"Tell me what he does the moment he reaches the corner." I pulled the Cheetah from its holster, ducked down behind the Goodwill box, and crouched with my back against the building. I held my gun in my left hand, the sap in my right.

"He's still coming," Mike said. "He's got his gun out. It's in his right hand. At his side. He's about three feet from the corner."

My pulse pounded as I crouched in my tiny dark corner. Every nerve in my body twitched. I felt as if I was about to go berserk.

"Two feet," Mike said.

My pulse pounded even harder. My right hand gripped the handle of the sap so tightly that my hand began to throb.

"He's reached the corner."

I took a deep, quiet breath. Then, tensing every muscle in my body, I prepared myself for the assault.

"He's coming your way," Mike said.

The shadow of the man approaching, reflected from the nearby spotlight, showed on the pavement a few feet directly in front of me.

Moments later, he was about to pass the box. Just then, he stopped. He'd no doubt spotted the Charger sitting next to the dumpster on the other side of the thoroughfare, about fifty feet away. His right arm came up, pointing the gun in that direction. I heard a slight rustling sound and saw him raise his left arm. It gripped a cell phone.

Then I heard Mike's voice, farther down, near the corner of the building: "Hey, cutie! Whatcha doin' over there?"

He spun around.

I slapped him smartly on the back of his skull.

Chapter 11

After checking the unconscious thug's pulse, I dropped his cell, stepped on it and ground it into the hard pavement. I grabbed his gun, removed the mag, and crossed the thoroughfare. Then I tossed the empty gun and mag into the bushes.

Mike came over just as I was heading back to the Goodwill box. "There's another one back there. He's coming this way."

"Of course he is."

"What do I do?"

"The same thing you did before."

"Gotcha." She vanished.

I hurried over to the Goodwill box. As before, I got out my gun and sap. Then I crouched behind the box and pressed my back against the block wall of the building.

Mike appeared again. "Ten feet from the corner." Then she vanished.

I took a deep breath and let the air back out slowly. My pulse began hammering again. I took another deep breath and fought to keep calm. It was a struggle, but I reminded myself that Mike was out there and would bail me out again.

"Five feet," Mike said, appearing on my right side.

Making sure I had a good range of motion, I positioned the sap about a foot from my right thigh.

"Two feet. One. Get ready."

The footsteps grew heavier and more rapid. The instant the second thug saw his buddy lying on the pavement, he stopped moving. Then, about five seconds later, he took half a dozen quick steps, until he'd cleared the outer corner of the box. He gazed at his fallen buddy for at least ten seconds. Something must have registered just then. An instant later, he jerked his face in my direction. His reactions were lightning quick. His arm came up the moment he spotted me. The black hole of the gun barrel positioned itself at my face.

"Hey, baby! What's goin' on?"

Cringing, he spun around in Mike's direction, and I was given a perfect shot of his back.

My sap sliced through the air, catching him squarely on the right temple. His gun flew out of his hand, clattering loudly on the pavement a few yards away. A gurgling sound escaped his throat, and he went down hard.

My heart raced. My body trembled, and I nearly dropped the sap. Luckily, my pants managed to stay dry. Once again, Mike had saved my life.

Two down. That meant one thug still wandering around, looking for the Charger.

Mike materialized on my left side. "The third guy's still in the sedan. He's on the phone."

"Any idea who he's talking to?"

"His boss, I suspect. They both know about the first guy's cell phone."

"He's not coming back here?"

"No. In fact—"

A cell buzzed. It wasn't mine. I bent and searched the guy's pockets. I found the cell in his jacket pocket. The display said *#1*. I knew better than answer it. I dropped it on the pavement at my feet and smashed it.

"Let me know what the driver's doing, okay?" I said to Mike.

"Be right back." She vanished.

I tossed the second gun and mag into the bushes on my way back to the Charger. The moment I opened the door and got behind the wheel, Mike appeared in the back seat. "He's headed toward this end of the mall," she said. "He's moving slow, so I figure we've got about two minutes, tops, to get away from here."

"Gotcha." I flicked on the ignition and backed up.

"What's going on?" Erin's classic deer-in-the-headlights expression practically lit up the dark interior. "Are you...*talking* to someone?"

"Later." This wasn't exactly the time to explain myself. Or, of course, Mike.

"Why won't you—"

"I said *later*." I took the Charger, without lights, down the back, in the opposite direction.

***

I had no trouble pulling out of the shopping center and getting back onto the main highway.

I saw no sign of a tail but knew better than let my guard down. My nerves were shot, and my pulse still thundered, but I managed to keep a firm hold on the wheel.

"What was all that about?" Erin asked.

"They just sent three armed goons after us." I figured this was probably the right time to start telling her what was going on.

"What happened?"

"I took care of them."

She was silent for a few moments. I figured she was trying to visualize what I'd just told her. And also trying to decide how to ask me what happened without sounding insulting. "All by yourself?" she finally asked.

"Explain that one," Mike said with a wry grin. "But please don't get me

involved. This girl's messed up enough."

I glanced at Erin and scowled. "See anyone else here? Besides you and me?"

She sat back. "I'm sorry. I guess I deserved that."

"You're getting much better at deflecting those," Mike said with a smile.

"I know," I said.

After a short silence, Erin said, "They were really armed? Really and truly *armed*? With *guns*?"

"Yep. They were loaded, too. With real bullets."

She went silent again. I could tell she was confused. A short time later, she asked, "How did you…what I mean is, how were you able to—"

"To do what?"

"Well…handle them…"

"Why are you so interested?"

Once again, she didn't speak right off. She was having trouble putting this all together.

"She can't understand what's happening," Mike said. "Be careful."

Erin turned and stared at me. "That guy who approached me at the mall the other day. He was...well, he seemed...*scary*."

"They usually are. Especially when they're armed. With guns."

"I don't mean to sound disrespectful, but—"

"You're about to say something that will be just that, aren't you?"

She just sat there, looking down at her hands in her lap. "Were they younger than you?"

"I guess you could say that."

"Taller?"

"A little."

"Well, the guy at the mall seemed more fit...more, well, capable. Were the three you just handled...well, were they like that?"

"What are you saying? You don't think I'm fit or capable?"

"I didn't say that at all."

"Are you saying I'm incompetent?"

"Not at all."

"What the hell *are* you trying to say, then?"

She shrugged. "I just thought, well, these guys all seem...frightening."

"They were."

She didn't respond.

"As I keep trying to tell you, I'm a professional."

81

"What does that have to do with—"

"Long story short, I know what I'm doing."

"But how does that explain how you handled three fit, armed guys?"

"I've been through this rodeo before."

"But there were *three* of them…"

"So?"

She shrugged. "You're…you're only one guy."

"And?"

"And you're not…well, you're not exactly twenty-five anymore…"

"Ouch…" Mike winced.

I decided not to let her have it. Not yet, anyway. "You're supposed to be intelligent, right?"

"I have a three-point-six average."

"Then if you're so smart, you should be able to figure out a few things. True, there were three of them. Also, I'm in this by myself. And yes, they're probably a couple of years younger than me. But I'm really good at this. I know their weak spots and I also know how to deal with them. Let's just leave it at that."

She didn't reply.

The rest of the trip was spent in silence.

Except for an occasional smirk from Mike.

Chapter 12

At seven-thirty, I stopped at the Park Place Motel a few blocks from Aloma.

The buildings were located just a few minutes west of Semoran, providing enough seclusion behind the well-trimmed bushes and palmettos to conceal the Charger.

I was exhausted, nervous, and frightened, and needed food and a few hours of uninterrupted sleep to get me through the night. It had been a rough day. I also badly needed a shower. If I didn't soon get a recharge, I didn't know how much longer I could go before I finally collapsed and took an unscheduled nap.

Before going inside the lobby, I made a quick call to Neil. I told him what had happened and where I'd left the two goons. As usual, he wasn't too wild about the news.

"They're not dead, are they?" he asked.

"Just out cold. I used a sap on both of them. And yeah, they were both armed."

"Any idea how they found out about this so damn soon?"

"I'm working on it."

"I'll ask Benton to send two men out there to pick them up. Maybe we can get something out of them after they sit in a couple of our interview rooms for two or three hours."

"Good luck with that. Especially if they work for Vega."

"Copy that. And you said Erin's okay?"

"She's fine. I'll be in touch."

I pocketed the cell, went inside, presented my card to purchase another double room and came back out just ten minutes later to collect the bags and Erin. We found the room easily. Then Erin hurried into the adjacent room to check it out.

I practically collapsed on the couch. I could hardly keep my eyes open, but when I started smelling the pizza again, my empty stomach protested, and I found myself instantly rejuvenated. Without pause I dove for the pizza box, opened it and bathed my senses in its heavenly vapors.

I was working on demolishing my second piece when Erin came out, grabbed two pieces of pizza, turned, and gave me an uneasy look. "Is it all right if I just go straight to bed? I'm pretty shaken up and tired."

"Go ahead. I'm gonna grab a couple of dozen quick z's myself just as soon as I finish this."

"What time will we be getting up tomorrow morning?"

"Early."

"And what time is that?"

"I figure around six, maybe seven o'clock."

Her frown made me realize that I'd forgotten that I was talking to a juvenile, one who probably didn't stir in the bed until long after eleven. "Seriously?"

It irritated me that she still wasn't following what was going on. "I've got to trade in the Charger."

"Why? It's a cool ride."

I shrugged. "It's been seen. By the bad guys. In other words, it's hot. Get it?"

"Uh-huh."

"You're sure?"

She nodded. "Just knock on the door when you're ready to go. I'll get up." Without another word she slipped back into her room and closed the door.

Just as I eagerly returned to my slice of pizza, Mike materialized before me, drifting directly over the coffee table. Once again, she had a grim expression on her beautiful face.

I stopped chewing. "What's up?"

"I think I might know how they found you," she said.

I put the uneaten piece back in the box and wiped the sauce from my chin with a paper towel. "How?"

"Erin."

I just looked at her. I didn't want to believe it, but I knew Mike. She wouldn't have said such a thing if it wasn't true. "Tell me the rest."

"She's on her cell phone right now."

I couldn't believe it. "She brought along a *cell phone*?"

A nod. "Right now, she talking to someone named Helena."

I jumped up from the couch, went over to the door and pounded on it.

It was ten seconds before she answered. The door stayed closed. "What *is* it?" she asked, her voice muffled.

"Open the door, Erin."

"W-What's going on? Did something hap—"

"Open the damned door!" I was in no mood for this. There wasn't time for bullshit. Now I knew what was going on. Erin had brought along her phone and it had obviously been tracked. There was no other way we could have been found so quickly. "I mean it!"

"Ralph, if there's something I need to know—"

"If you don't open this door in two seconds, I'm gonna break it down. One…"

The knob turned. The door opened slowly.

I pushed it open the rest of the way and marched over to the bed, where the opened suitcase lay. I began rummaging through her clothes.

"What are you doing?" She rushed over and stood very close, her face inches from my shoulder. Her eyes were huge; she was angry and confused. "Why are you doing this?"

The cell phone in her left hand jumped right out at me. It took every ounce of self-control I had to keep from snatching it from her and shoving it down her throat. "Why in heaven's name do you have a cell phone?"

She gawked at it as if she'd forgotten she was holding it. "Ralph, if you're going to make a big issue about this…"

"Give it to me." My self-control began crumbling.

"W-Why do you want my cell phone?"

I had to take a deep breath before I was able to get the words out coherently. "Give it to me. Now. Right now."

"But why?"

That was all I could take. I snatched it from her, tossed it to the floor and stomped on it.

She stood there shaking, her chin dangling, her hands outstretched. She looked like I'd just killed her beloved dog. Or her newborn child. Her face splashed crimson. I thought she was going to have a heart attack. "*Why did you do that?*"

I grabbed a handful of her clothes from her suitcase and tossed them onto the mattress. What I saw lying underneath them made my blood boil. I groaned. And gritted my teeth. And fought like hell to refrain from pulling out my hair. In that same moment, I could feel what was left of my self-control scurrying away.

There they were, lying right there. Two more glaring signs of why this case was going down the tubes so rapidly.

A laptop. And an iPad.

"Uh-oh…" from Mike.

I could feel every muscle in my body quivering. I was staring at a very intelligent twenty-year-old female college student. A young woman who was the niece of a very good friend of mine. A friend who was a cop. A cop who would have gladly stopped a bullet for this girl. This naïve, immature girl, who had done exactly what every other young person like her, male or female, would have done in similar circumstances.

She'd not only put her own life in danger, but she'd also included me in her naïve stupidity.

"Why didn't you tell me you brought all this with you?"

"Why did you destroy my cell phone?" She'd totally ignored my question and turned her full attention to a much more important issue. She couldn't take her eyes off the mangled mess I'd made on the floor. Her body trembled. Her arms hung tensely at her sides. Her hands were balled into tight fists. Her face was flushed, her eyes wide-open and twitching. "I've had that phone for *two years!*"

"You should have told me—and your uncle—and Detective Benson—that you brought all this with you."

Still gawking at the mess, she chose once again to ignore the most urgent issue. "I had all my photos on that phone. Picnics. Parties. School functions. My prom. Homecoming. Family get-togethers." She slowly raised her face and glared at me. She appeared possessed. If I hadn't been so enraged, I would have been frightened.

"You ruined my cell phone! You destroyed all my memories! You're a—"

"Before you start the ball rolling with what'll no doubt turn into a sloppy name-calling tirade, just keep one thing in mind."

Once again she demonstrated to both me and Mike that she wasn't listening to anything I said. "I *hate* you! I—"

"Those memories of yours almost cost us our lives." I didn't care about her stupid cell phone. The damned thing had enabled the bad guys to track us. I'd almost been killed in the process, and I wasn't about to let her off the hook.

"I'll *never* forgive you for this! I'm gonna tell my uncle, and then you're gonna buy me a brand-new cell phone!"

"She's not listening to you," Mike said.

"Yeah. I know."

"Whaddya mean, you know? Did you *hear* me? Are you *listening* to me? Don't you realize what you've *done*?"

I had to remind myself that I couldn't strangle her or tie and gag her and dump her into the trunk of the Charger. It would have made my day, but Neil wouldn't have liked it. At all.

"You're talking loud enough for our neighbors to hear you. I'm three feet away. Of course I can hear you. And yes, I know exactly what I've done."

"Well, what have you got to say about all this?"

I moved closer to her laptop and iPad. "Does this stuff have phone capabilities?"

She cringed, her gaze switching nervously from me to her laptop and iPad. "W-Why?"

"Does it or doesn't it?"

Her eyes grew. She took a breath and put her hands on her hips. "What difference does it make?"

Mike had disappeared. The way things were going, I figured this wasn't a good thing. "I guess I'll take that as a yes."

"Why should it even matter?" she asked.

Something told me that whatever I said would be wrong.

"Well? Are you gonna answer me?" She was still glaring. "Or are you gonna just stand there looking stupid, like an idiot?"

Mike suddenly materialized in the doorway, looking grim again. "There's someone outside, snooping around."

My pulse racing, I put my index finger up to my lips.

Erin blinked. "*Now* what are you doing? What the hell does *that* mean?"

I gave her one of my meanest expressions, which worked in most circumstances. However, Erin was much too upset and enraged to pay attention. So, to give my expression a little more clout, I moved closer to her, stopping when we were just a few inches away from one another. "It means," I whispered tensely, "shut the hell up."

She was about to say something when I pulled out my gun. She immediately clamped her mouth shut and backed away.

"Is he armed?" I asked Mike.

"I think so."

"What's he doing?"

"He's checking out the Charger."

"Who are you talking to?" Erin had apparently gotten over her mad and returned to her frightened mode. Good thing. I knew it would be impossible to explain to Neil why I'd been forced to deck his favorite niece when I was supposed to be protecting her.

"My contact." I moved toward the open doorway.

"Where…is he?" She nervously scanned the room.

"Don't worry about it." I wasn't in the mood for any more of her nonsense.

"W-Where…are you going?" she whispered tensely. "What's happening? Why're you acting so weird?"

"Stay here." I made a move to close her door.

She blocked me. "You're not *leaving* me, are you?"

"Just for a minute."

"But—"

"I'll be back, okay?"

Still shaking, she watched me edgily as I quietly closed her door.

I crossed the outer room and flicked off all the lights. "Mike? Where are you?" I whispered.

"Right here, beside you."

"Go on out there and tell me what he's doing, okay?"

"Be right back."

I stood behind the door, my gun and sap ready as I listened to the heavy silence. I couldn't hear anything. Luckily, Erin wasn't making any noise. If we were lucky, she'd stay quiet and not make this situation any worse. Her equipment had gotten us into enough trouble. Once I eliminated whoever was snooping around outside, I was going to have to trash her laptop and iPad. I knew what complications that would cause, but I just didn't have any other option. I figured it was much better to have a college girl mad at me than get us both killed by trying to stay on her good side.

Mike came right back. Although I still couldn't see her, I heard her voice. "He just opened the driver's door of the Charger. He's bent over the front seat on the driver's side, looking for stuff. He's got a penlight. If you sneak outside within the next ten seconds, he's in the perfect position for you to sucker him."

"Thanks." I slipped off my shoes. Then I quietly opened the door, snuck outside and went over to the Charger.

The sight made me want to laugh.

The man couldn't have been more vulnerable. His butt was in the perfect position. Without hesitation, I kicked him between the legs, driving a harsh, high-pitched gasp from him. His body arched, and he hit his head sharply on the dash.

Just as he tried backing out, I brought down the sap directly onto the back of his head.

He moaned weakly and went slack.

Chapter 13

After dumping the man in the trunk of the Charger, I drove over to the dumpster behind the motel, parked next to it and opened the trunk.

Using my penlight, I examined him. He was still unconscious, and the back of his head was bleeding. I made a mental note to call Neil about this once I'd taken Erin to a safe place.

I pocketed the penlight, grabbed the man by his arms and pulled him out of the trunk. Then, grasping him by the wrists, I dragged him closer to the side of the container and left him there.

Erin was hiding in the closet in the adjoining room when I got back to the hotel room. "You okay in there?" I whispered.

"What's going on?" she whispered back.

"I've got one thing to do. Wait here another minute, okay?"

"Are we safe? Can we—"

"I'll be right back." I went over to her bag and removed her laptop and iPad. Then I put her clothes back in the suitcase and took the bag and her equipment outside. Once I'd placed her bag in the back seat and the electronic equipment in the trunk, I went back inside.

She still hadn't come out of the closet.

"You still all right?"

"When can I come out?"

I opened the door. "We've got to move quickly."

She came out and looked for her suitcase. "Where's my stuff?"

"I packed it all up and put it in the car."

She gawked at me. "You...packed my stuff?"

"Sure did."

"When...why did you—"

"Not time to waste. C'mon." I gestured to the door. "We've got to go."

Without further protest, she followed me out to the Charger and got in. I got behind the wheel, pulled out and drove directly to the dumpster. I popped open the trunk and got out. Then, while her vision was blocked by the opened trunk, I grabbed her laptop and iPad from the trunk, opened the heavy plastic lid of the dumpster and tossed the equipment inside.

***

At 8:00, we pulled back onto the main highway.

I realized right then that Erin was glaring again. "What did you toss in that dumpster?"

I didn't reply.

From the back seat, Mike said, "You might have to chloroform her once you tell her. A straitjacket might even help."

I nodded. "I know."

"You know what?" Erin was gawking at me.

"I know what I tossed in that dumpster."

"Good. Now you can tell me."

"Guess."

94

"This isn't funny, Ralph. I'm *so* not amused by all this."

"Really?"

"Yes. Really. Totally."

"You're not amused by the fact that people have been stalking us and trying to kill us all day? I'm really surprised. For a moment I thought you might be thinking this was all one big game."

"I know this isn't a game, Ralph."

"I don't think you actually realize what's going on."

"And how'd you come up with that?"

"The fact that you've been carrying around a traceable cell phone. And a traceable laptop. And a traceable iPad. And instead of thanking me for saving your life—not once, but several times—all you want to do is yell at me for destroying your cell phone and tossing your laptop and iPad into the dumpster."

"You *what*?"

"You heard me."

"You…you actually…you tossed my *laptop* and *iPad*? In the *dumpster*?"

"Now you got it."

"Really?"

"Scout's honor."

"You…you *idiot*…"

"You're welcome."

She didn't reply. She just sat there, simmering, as if she'd turned into a pile of burning coals. Then she clenched her fists and began shaking her head. Moments later, she moaned and jerked in the seat.

95

She looked like she was having a fit. I was tempted to stop the car, pull over and give her CPR. But I was afraid she'd kill me before I could do anything.

"You okay?" I asked.

"Of *course* I'm not okay, you idiot!"

"What's wrong?"

"What's wrong? What's wrong?"

"Let's go with that instead."

"You idiot. You moron. You dumbass. You—"

"You could throw in a shithead and a couple of assholes while you're at it."

She just glared.

"Let me ask you a question," I said.

She still didn't reply.

"It's really important."

She shrugged. "Go ahead. You're a moron, but you're gonna ask anyway, so just ask away."

"Didn't your uncle mention your cell phone?"

"Whaddya mean?"

"Didn't he tell you to leave it home? As well as the laptop and iPad?"

"What if he did?"

"Did he?"

A reluctant nod.

"Well, then? Why didn't you do it?"

She was silent for a few moments. "He knows how much I need my cell and laptop. I could've left the iPad—"

"Why didn't you? And why didn't you listen to your uncle?"

She shrugged. "Like I just said, I need my stuff. I feel naked without my cell."

96

"There's something wrong here," Mike said.

"Yeah. I know."

"You know what?" Erin asked.

"Just thinking out loud."

She went back to glaring. Then she turned away and moaned.

About a minute later, she began shaking her head again, but slower this time. "I just can't believe you actually *did* that! I can't believe you tossed technological equipment worth three thousand dollars into a dumpster! Are you stupid? Are you insane?"

"Probably both, if you ask certain people."

"How *could* you? How could you just toss my valuable personal stuff in a dumpster?"

"I don't know. Call me stupid—oh wait, you just did. You also called me a dumbass, an idiot, and a—"

"I know what I called you, so don't be cute…or silly—or whatever you wanna call yourself after you've done something stupid and really costly. Just answer my question, dammit!"

"All righty. Here's your answer, in a nutshell. I guess I kind of figured our lives were worth more than what a cellphone, laptop and iPad would cost to replace."

She gave me the strangest look. It made me feel like I had cockroaches coming out of my ears. "I don't believe you! I can't believe what you just did! Are you from this planet, even?"

"Sometimes I wonder about that myself."

"How could you even consider doing that? I know you're old and messed up and stupid and probably a whole bunch of other things, but even someone like you can understand how expensive that stuff is. That laptop cost me—"

"I'm only interested in how much that crap *almost* cost."

"What are you talking about now?"

"There was another goon outside our motel room. Whether you know it or not, he tracked us. He was searching the car when I got him."

"Another *goon*?"

"Good. You're paying attention."

"Are you sure?"

"Positive."

"I mean, really and truly positive?"

"I know a goon when I see one."

"And by the way, that contact of yours. How come I didn't hear anything?"

"What did you expect to hear?"

"I didn't even see you talking into anything."

"I was wearing an earpiece. Haven't you ever seen *Person of Interest*? How about *24*? Or *any* TV shows that specialize in technology?"

"Of course I've seen them—"

"There's your answer, then."

"Who *is* this contact? Why haven't you mentioned him before?"

"I didn't think it was necessary."

"This concerns me, doesn't it?"

"Yeah. It concerns you. My contact doesn't. And by the way, he's actually a she."

"Your contact is a *she*?"

"You really are paying attention, aren't you?"

She sat back in her seat and crossed her arms. She didn't say anything or even shake her head this time, but I could tell she was furious. But it didn't matter. I had to ditch her equipment in a hurry, and I didn't have time to be diplomatic. Facing four goons in the last couple of hours was just too much. If it hadn't been for Mike, I'd be dead, and the goons would have snatched Erin.

The next couple of miles were spent in tense silence. Then, as we went through another four-way intersection, Erin asked, "Where are we going?"

"I'm taking us to another motel."

"*Another* one?"

"Unless you'd like to spend the night in this car with me."

She groaned and looked down at her lap.

"I guess she doesn't like your company so much anymore," Mike said.

"Yeah."

"What?" Erin turned and glared.

"I said—"

"I heard what you said. I'd just like to know why you said it."

"I'm talking to my contact again. She's wondering where we're going, too."

Erin moved a little closer. She was no doubt trying to spot an earpiece. "I don't see anything in your ear."

"I've got two of them, actually. One on this side and one just like it on the other."

"Then it's in your other ear?"

"Go to the head of the class. I'd show you, but that would require me turning my head at a really painful angle, and I'm more interested in reaching the next motel alive rather than dead, or all messed up."

"Are you always this sarcastic?"

"Only when I'm awake—or with someone causing me problems."

"*I'm* causing *you* problems?"

"Gee, I wish *I'd* said that."

"How could I be causing you problems?"

I couldn't believe she'd asked such a ridiculous question. "You're not serious. Tell me you're not serious. Tell me you just didn't ask me the most absurd question I've heard in a long, long time."

Her big blue eyes filled their sockets. "I'm totally deadly serious. And I'd really appreciate it if you'd just stop insulting me and being so condescending. So please answer my question."

"You're sure you want an answer to that?"

"*Please…*"

"Well, to answer your *serious* question about why I just said that you're causing me problems, let me say this. I just saved your life a couple of times, and all you seem to care about is that I trashed your cell and dumped your laptop and iPad."

"And you don't see why I pitched a fit about that?"

"I *know* why you pitched the fit."

"Then what's the problem?"

"I just kind of figured that you'd prefer losing a couple of thousand dollars' worth of disposable electronic equipment over losing a couple of your *non*disposable fingers, or your hand—which, I assume, you probably value as well. Or, in a worst-case scenario, your life—which, I also assume, you value just as much."

She sat back in her seat and stared straight ahead.

"I guess you finally managed to shut her up," Mike said.

"I finally did."

"What did your contact just say?" Erin asked.

"It was just a technical question."

"Is she a detective, too?"

"You could say that."

"Where is she?"

"Not far."

Erin turned and glanced at her side mirror. "You mean she could be in another car, following us?"

"She's never very far away."

"What's her name?"

"I'm beginning to feel very strange about this," Mike said. "I've never liked being talked about. Especially while I'm sitting right there, listening and watching and no one even knows I'm there."

"Why do you care?" I asked Erin.

"Just curious."

"The less you know, the better."

"Whaddya mean?"

"It's better for you. Healthier, too."

101

"How can it be healthier?"

I was beginning to wonder if Neil knew just how naïve his niece really was. "If these people manage to find us and take you away, you're a helluva lot better off, not knowing very much. Especially if they decide to get a little rough when they ask you certain questions."

She went silent again.

"I think you just scared her," Mike said.

"Good thing," I said.

Erin watched me but didn't say anything.

Chapter 14

A few miles later, as we approached another four-way light, Erin asked, "Are we gonna be stopping soon? I've got to use the restroom."

I glanced at the clock on the dash. It was after 8:30. Traffic had thinned, and since dinnertime was long gone, I decided that we could relax for a little while. "There's an Awful Waffle about a mile or so down this stretch. We can stop there. I could seriously use some coffee."

"That sounds great."

Once the light changed and we followed the thinning stream down the straight stretch, I pulled into the turn-off lane. The moment I spotted a gap, I cut across the highway, pulled into the front entrance of the eatery and drove all the way down the half-empty lot.

I parked on the other side of a super-cab Dodge truck, which totally concealed the Charger from view of the main drag. We went in through the front entrance and I slid into a corner booth close to the door while Erin crossed the long, bright room, where the restrooms were marked at the far end.

There were only about a dozen others sitting on stools and at tables. The slender brunette waitress was busy handling things but didn't look too stressed. After delivering a dinner order to the middle-aged couple three tables down, she came

103

over to my booth and asked if I wanted coffee. I nodded. She turned and hurried back to her station.

"Want me to stick my head in the ladies' room and see what your charge is doing?" Mike asked.

"My charge?"

She smiled. "I was trying to be polite."

"Brat sounds more appropriate. Or bitch. Or serious problem child. Arrogant Millennial would suffice as well."

"As I said…"

"She was so nice and reasonably mature when I first met her. What the hell happened?"

"She was just dealt a heavy dose of reality."

"The goons-stalking-her part? Or the tragic loss of her cellphone, laptop and iPad?"

"Probably a combination of both. Kids her age can't deal with anything they're not familiar with. I'll bet she's been spoiled all her life."

"She sure acts like she has been."

"The cell phone is her generation's lifeline. They can't function without it. For someone of your generation, it would be like slicing your jugular."

"That's sad. And seriously stupid."

"I agree, but that's the way it is."

"I saved her life. All she cares about is that stupid cell. And that stupid laptop. And that stupid iPad."

"As I said, they're all like that now."

"I know. That's what pisses me off. Frightens me, too."

Mike nodded. "I'm not too wild about it, either. But since I'm dead, it no longer concerns me."

"They walk around, talking and texting one another about the most ridiculous things. They could care less about the rest of the world, what's going on around them, or even what's happening under their very noses. You could walk right up to any one of them, stick a gun in their face, and they probably wouldn't even pay attention or stop the texting as you calmly blew their head off."

Mike just shrugged.

"But that bit about Neil really has me baffled. He would've most certainly told her to leave all her stuff at home. He knows what a GPS would do to this operation."

"I don't think she told you the whole truth. I think she's definitely keeping something from you."

"You're right. All I have to do now is figure out what the hell it is—"

The waitress brought me my coffee. "Ready to order?"

"I'll wait until my...niece...comes back, thanks."

She hurried back to the counter to pick up another order.

I put sugar in my coffee and stirred. Then I focused on the opposite end of the room, where the rest rooms were. No Erin. It was already several minutes, but I knew better than try and second-guess a young person. Especially a female. I sipped my coffee. "Think she's okay in there?"

Mike shook her head. "I don't know. I can't tell from here."

"Would you mind very much?"

"I'll give the room a quick peek." She vanished.

I had more coffee and sat back. I was tired. My shoulders and back were sore from the scuffles. And my being pissed at Erin didn't help the situation one bit. Hopefully, she'd use that superior brain Neil had been bragging about and figure out what was happening. Maybe she'd finally see that the cost of replacing a cell, a laptop, and an iPad wasn't really that much in the great scheme of things, especially when her life—as well as mine—had been in jeopardy. I just wanted her to demonstrate some common sense and realize that in spite of my faults and my sarcasm, I was just trying to keep her safe.

But I had to find out why she deliberately ignored Neil's advice and brought her equipment with her.

I had more coffee and tried to relax. I entertained a brief heavenly vision of finding another motel room, collapsing on the bed and sleeping through the night. Maybe the worst was over. Maybe the bad guys would see what they were up against and call it a day. Maybe they'd report back to their boss and would be told to try again tomorrow. Or maybe they'd finally realized that Erin really didn't have what they wanted.

And one day, maybe pigs would fly.

I realized that I'd just reverted into a completely ridiculous, unrealistic Pollyanna attitude, but I was tired and wanted to think of things that wouldn't sour my mood.

After more internal struggling, I told myself to stop agonizing over all this. I'd managed to save Erin, and once we'd both enjoyed a good night's sleep, we'd be facing another day. Maybe a much better one.

There was always the chance that Neil would find out what was going on. Then he'd call to tell me that the bad guys had been nabbed and that it was okay for me to bring Erin back to the Station.

Mike materialized beside me in the seat. I could tell that she wasn't pleased.

"Please tell me I don't have anything to worry about," I whispered, hoping against hope that I was worrying over nothing.

"I wish I could."

I put down my cup. "Go ahead, then. Let me have it. Tell me what she's doing in there."

"I can't."

"Why not?"

"She's not there."

"What?"

"She's gone."

"Gone?"

"Gone."

"You mean—"

"Not there. Absent. Missing. Disappeared. To put it simply, she's no longer in our sights."

"Dammit!" A hundred different images flashed in my head all at once. Erin slipping out through the back. Someone helping Erin slip out through the back. Someone knocking Erin out and carrying her out through the back. Two guys involved, one of

107

them chloroforming her while the other kept the door open. Three bad guys involved. Or maybe four. Neil standing in front of me, his arms crossed, his scowl burning into mine as he said, "How the hell did you let her slip through your fingers?"

More images swept past, none of them comforting or optimistic. Whatever had happened wasn't good, no matter how I looked at it. In spite of my instincts, my experience, and even Mike's invaluable help, I'd lost Erin.

But maybe it wasn't too late. Maybe it had only happened a moment ago. Or two. Or even three. "Did you check out back?"

"I thought I'd give you the bad news first."

Groaning, I stood up, dropped a five on the counter and ran outside.

Mike stayed right beside me. "What do you want me to do now?"

My pulse raced as I stared at the length of the building. A thin strip of woods ran perpendicular to the building, about forty feet from the edge of the paved lot. There were some pines, then what looked like a subdivision on the other side. The pines stood very close together, preventing a vehicle from slipping through. The woods appeared too dense and overgrown for a body to elbow through. Two men carrying a woman, even one as slender as Erin, would have trouble maneuvering through the thick brush.

To me, this meant one thing. Their escape route rested on going around the length of the building and getting away using the front entrance.

Since I'd been sitting near a window, I would have seen some sort of activity. But I hadn't. However, I'd been sitting with my back facing this side of the building. The other side of the room was lined with windows as well, but the customers occupying the booths made it difficult for me to have seen anyone sneaking about. Customer parking was limited on this side to two aisles, but the lot on the other side of the building provided ample spaces. The people who had taken Erin could have carried her next door, dumped her in the trunk of a vehicle and gotten away through the entrance next door.

But what if they *hadn't* gotten away yet?

That possibility raised the hairs on the back of my neck. I turned to Mike. "Go around the corner. If someone's in back, let me know right off."

"I'm on it." She vanished.

Taking a deep breath, I crept toward the back, between the building and the front of the line of parked vehicles. My hand slid underneath my jacket and gripped the cool handle of the Cheetah in its holster. I could feel the sweat on my hand and on the back of my neck, but I couldn't let that distract me. I forced myself to concentrate.

My senses in overload, I kept moving. I couldn't hear anything but the heavy traffic thirty yards behind me, but I knew from experience that silence could be very deceptive and could switch from friend to foe in a heartbeat.

Just as I was about to reach the corner of the building, Mike appeared a few feet in front of me.

Her expression this time was worse than grim. She was frightened. But what alarmed me was that she wasn't looking directly at me. She'd shifted her gaze on something behind me, a foot or so to my left.

My instinct kicked in the instant I heard a soft footstep on the pavement close behind me.

Before I could turn around, something hard cracked me on the back of my skull.

Chapter 15

A dull throbbing in the back of my head woke me.

I opened my eyes and found myself squinting at total darkness. The air was musty and damp and smelled faintly of mothballs. I sighed. A black hood had been slipped over my head.

Dammit. The very thought of this happening to me again infuriated me. The same damned thing had happened just a few years ago, when one of Vega's men had brought me to see Vega—

Vega. I shuddered the moment I thought that I was about to talk to the bastard again.

Forcing the terror away, I struggled to think rationally. A hood didn't necessarily mean Vega, did it? All the hood really meant was that whoever had slipped it over my head didn't want me seeing anything.

I needed to collect myself and assess my new surroundings. I was lying on my right side with the hard floor vibrating beneath me. My arms were pulled behind my back. The fact that I couldn't pull them apart told me they'd been fastened together at the wrists. Since my hands and fingers were almost numb, I figured nylon cord or zip ties had been used. After very little experimentation with my legs, I discovered the same thing went for my ankles.

Terrific. Knocked out, hooded, tied up, and tossed in the trunk of a moving vehicle.

The fact that I'd been placed in this same frightening predicament before irritated me. It made me realize that once I'd gotten out of this, I needed to get back to my apartment, relax on the couch with some Jack and re-evaluate my future. I wasn't getting any younger, and my bones and joints no longer responded as they'd done not long before. At this rate, I'd be a walking textbook of cracked joints and badly healed bones by the time I hit fifty. I'd been slugged in the head several times and feared the day would come when just one more well-placed blow would prove too much. I wasn't quite ready to spend the rest of my days in a wheelchair while some bored nurse hand-fed me a regimen of daily meds and stewed prunes.

That dark, dismal thinking would just have to wait. Right now, the most important thing was to figure out my options. I just hoped I had one that wouldn't make this situation any worse.

My first reaction was to find out if Mike was anywhere close.

Since the hood prevented me from seeing anything, I decided to refrain from talking. If one of my abductors was close by, I didn't want them knowing I'd come to. I just groaned and hoped it would lead to something.

The steady hum of the vehicle was all I heard.

In case Mike was close and hadn't caught that first groan, I turned my head and did it again.

Her voice dispelled most of my fears. "I'm here."

Before I could whisper anything to her, she said, "Don't say anything. You're in the back of a gray van, and your charge is right here with you. Behind you. About two feet away."

I gave a slight nod.

Just then, I heard Erin's voice. She sounded very close behind me. "Are you awake yet?"

"Erin?"

"Of course."

"You're here, too?"

"Of course I'm here."

"Are you tied up, like me?"

"Of course."

"Are you hooded?"

"Are you?"

"I asked you first."

"They stuck some gross-smelling cloth thing over my head—if that's what you mean."

"That's what I mean."

"You, too?"

"You could say that."

"She's lying," Mike said. "She's not tied up and she's not hooded. She's sitting on a pillow, watching you."

I felt a sudden chill climbing up my back.

If Erin was lying, this meant many things, none of them good or promising. It also meant that she'd been lying to me about other things, as well.

It made me wonder exactly what the hell was going on.

113

I decided to keep calm and act clueless. The simple fact that she'd just lied to me about her status suggested that she was very likely an important part of this program. And if I wanted to find out just what the program was—as well as get out of it alive—I needed to stay collected and smart.

Most of all, I needed to do whatever Mike told me. As usual, Mike was my eyes. But in this case, she was everything.

"So they got you, too?" I asked Erin.

"Good tactic," Mike said.

"Obviously," Erin said.

"The Awful Waffle?"

"Someone was waiting for me when I came out of the ladies' room."

"See who it was?"

"They got me from behind and put some sort of medicine-smelling wet cloth in my face."

"Probably chloroform."

"It made me sick when I finally woke up in this stupid van."

"Are you in any pain?"

A pause. "I've probably got some bruises when they shoved me in here."

"Another lie," Mike said.

I was beginning to distrust Erin even more than moments ago.

"So what's happened? Where are we? And are you still in touch with your contact?"

"I haven't heard from her in a while. I think I lost my earpiece when they roughed me up."

"Maybe, maybe not."

114

"You think I still might have it?"

"You might be lying to me. I don't know about you anymore."

"Whaddya mean?"

"I know my uncle trusts you and all, but I honestly don't think I can."

"Good one," Mike said. "She's tossing this in your court."

"Why can't you?"

"For one thing, you destroyed my phone."

I groaned. "Are you still upset about that?"

"What do *you* think? And my laptop. And my iPad. Besides, you were supposed to be protecting me. What part of this don't you understand? What part of it doesn't register with you?"

"You can stop this crap anytime you wish. I told you why I did it. So why don't we just leave it at that?"

I heard her sigh.

"You still haven't told me why you deliberately ignored what your uncle told you to do."

"I've already told you—"

"You told me how much you need your stuff. You didn't say exactly why your stuff is more important than your life. Or mine…"

She went silent. After about fifteen seconds, she said, "So what about your contact? Does she know we've been kidnapped? Where is she?"

"She really knows how to change the subject," Mike said.

"I don't know where she is," I told Erin. "I don't seem to be able to do too much about contacting her right now, if you know what I mean."

She didn't reply right off. Then, after a short silence, she said, "Maybe she's closer than you think. She might even be trying to get someone here to rescue us. What do you really think is going on?"

I fought hard to figure out what I could tell her that wouldn't make this more dangerous for me.

"Tell her I'm having trouble keeping with your frequency," Mike said. "If she thinks you're on your own, she might open up. She's obviously here with you to find out what you know. There was a guy in this van with her before you woke up. I'm not sure, but I think he's that Johnny guy your rude police buddy's been looking for. Blond hair? Blue eyes?"

That was definitely something I didn't want to hear right now.

"Well?" Erin sounded anxious.

I took a deep breath to force myself to stay calm and not say anything that would get me killed. "I don't think I lost the piece when they roughed me up, so there could be some sort of technical problem making it more difficult for her to transmit."

"Like what?"

"She could be in heavy traffic, so she can't get a good reading. You there? Do you copy?" I waited a few seconds. "Nothing."

"You really wear an earpiece?"

"Why do you ask?"

"She's watching you closely," Mike said. "They checked before and didn't find one, of

116

course. I honestly don't know what you can tell her."

"Just curious."

"Well, it might have been knocked out when they hit me over the head."

"What if it didn't?"

"Then I'll eventually hear from her."

"Maybe it did fall out. Maybe they already checked when they knocked you out and didn't find one."

"What would make them check?" I decided to put a little pressure on her.

A short pause. "Isn't that what these guys do? Don't they frisk you and check all your pockets and clothes? Your shoes, even? The whole nine yards?"

"Normally. But I'm not sure about these guys."

"Whaddya mean?"

"Some outfits don't care much about things like earpieces. The guys who took us are obviously working for important people who dictate their every move. All they'd care about would be my cell and any hardware I've got. I'm sure they took my gun and my knife, as well as the cell your uncle gave me. That's all they'd be concerned about."

"Nice touch," Mike said. "If she says anything else, it'll give her away. She's smart enough to know that."

She was quiet for several moments. Then she said, "Where do you think they're taking us?"

"Don't you know?"

"How would *I* know?"

"Well, Grayson's behind this, isn't he?"

117

"Why would Johnny be behind this?"

"He's your boyfriend, isn't he?"

"You definitely twanged a nerve," Mike said. "Right now, she's glaring at you. And her hands have turned into fists."

She sighed. "Why would you think he's my boyfriend?"

"That's what this is all about, isn't it? Your being tangled up with Grayson? His ties to Vega?"

"Who's *that*?"

"I think she's telling the truth," Mike said. "She actually looks very confused right now."

"You've never heard of Arturo Vega?"

"Who is *he*? And why would you think I'd be involved with someone who'd drug me, put a hood over my head and take me somewhere in the back of a van?"

"She actually looks frightened," Mike said. "It's probably just an act, but I think you'd better back off a little until you find out what's going on."

"Just a guess," I said to Erin.

"Well, your guess is obviously wrong."

"Sorry about that."

"Why say it, then?"

"I'm a detective. To work a case, I often have to get down and dirty. Most of the time, I use my gut and go strictly on hunches. Many times, my hunches are wrong. But I have to go this way, or I'll never be able to figure out anything."

"Well, if you think Johnny's tangled up with anyone who'd do something like this, you're wrong."

"She sounds pretty definite about this," Mike said. "Especially for someone who told you she doesn't know Grayson very well."

Mike was right. In fact, she was so right that I almost figured out why Erin was here with me. And not tied up. And not hooded.

"How long have you known Grayson?"

"Not long. Why?"

"Just a question."

"Well, I don't see why my meeting a nice-looking guy at a nightclub and having a drink with him would involve all this."

"All what?"

"This thing right out of a suspense movie. Someone approaching me at the Mall. Showing me his gun. Then disappearing when my friends showed up."

"Uh-huh…"

"You sound like…like you don't believe me."

"Just trying to put a few details together. But do go on."

"I just don't see why all this is happening. That thing at the Mall, then your showing up and driving me to two motels, then totally destroying my cell, laptop, and iPad."

"I've already told you several times why I did that."

"Right. Something about some bad guys using my stuff to track us."

"I was right, wasn't I?"

"Huh? Oh. Yes. You were right."

"You don't sound convinced."

119

"I'm really not."

"Why not?"

"You trashed my equipment, but they tracked us down anyway."

"And?"

"This tells me you didn't really have to destroy anything, did you? Now it looks like you did all that for nothing."

"With the latest high-tech equipment, once you grab enough coordinates, you don't need a GPS anymore."

She didn't respond.

"In other words," I said, "the damage was already done. They'd used your hardware to track us. But I didn't know they were closing in even after I'd immobilized three of their men. If I had, I wouldn't have even bothered doing anything to your equipment."

"Well, what are you gonna do about it?"

"About what?"

"Whaddya think? The two of us are tied up, blindfolded, and being taken somewhere. You must have *some* plan you're working on right now to get us out of this."

"Now how would I possibly have something like that going on?"

"You're a detective, right?"

"What does that have anything to do with—"

"You're always telling me how good you are. How experienced. How professional. Well, now's the time to use all that experience of yours to get us out of this. My uncle even paid you to keep me safe.

In other words, since we've both been kidnapped and have no idea where we are or who is doing this, you accepted money under false pretenses. I'm twenty years old. I'm much too young to die, dammit."

"Now she's sounding pathetic," Mike said. "If I were you, I'd give her something to think about. Something vague, yet very tempting."

"Well, since you've mentioned it, I might have some sort of plan in the works."

"Really? What is it?"

"Watch it, now," Mike said. "She just pulled something out of the front of her shirt. It looks like some sort of electronic device. If I'm right, you're being recorded. I'll even bet someone's been listening since the moment she started talking to you."

This made me even angrier. I knew I should have suspected it, but the throbbing in my skull had been very distracting. It had subsided somewhat, making things much clearer. I fully realized that Mike's assessment of the situation was not to be taken lightly.

"I'd rather not say right now," I told Erin.

"Why not?"

"This van, or truck…well, it could be bugged."

Mike laughed. "She just turned three shades of white, then grabbed her bug and stuck it back in her shirt."

"Wh-What makes you say that?"

"Just one of those hunches I told you about."

121

Mike said, "She just got a text. She brought a cell out of her pocket and now she's reading it. It says, "We're approaching the drop-off. If you can't get anything else from him, hold off. More time later.""

"Well," she said, "I suggest you start thinking faster. I kind of think that whoever's taking us somewhere might be getting really close to our destination—wherever that is."

About half a minute later, the big vehicle slowed down, turned, and pulled onto a bumpy road.

"How about that?" I told her. "You were right."

She didn't respond.

"You're good," I added. "It's almost like you've got a sixth sense."

She still didn't reply.

"You definitely struck another nerve," Mike said.

Chapter 16

The van slowed down again and eased to a stop.

I heard the grinding of gears, and then the vehicle backed up slowly. The van continued backing up for about ten seconds before stopping again.

My curiosity about our whereabouts surfaced once again. I figured about twenty minutes had passed from the time I'd come to. This didn't tell me anything, since each turn the van made had disoriented me even more. And since I had no idea how long I'd been unconscious, this made my predicament even more complicated. For all I knew, we could be in Gainesville, Tampa, Miami, or Cocoa Beach.

The instant the vehicle stopped vibrating, Mike said, "We're in Kissimmee, just a mile or so from One-Ninety. They've brought you to a brand-new hotel, but it isn't fully open yet. There are maybe a dozen cars parked out front, but I haven't seen anyone else around."

"I'm getting scared," Erin whispered. She'd obviously moved closer to where I lay. Possibly to gain my sympathy.

"She's convincing," Mike said. "I'll give her that."

"Don't worry," I whispered back. I hoped Erin wouldn't be able to figure out that I knew she was faking it. "We'll get out of this okay."

"Do you really have a plan? I mean really?"

"Working on it."

"Can you tell me about it yet?"

"It's not quite ready yet…"

"Please hurry. I'm about to come out of my skin."

"I'm surprised you can't hear her filing her nails," Mike said flatly.

My anger flared once again. I lay there and forced myself not to lose my composure.

Then I heard the ignition being switched off.

The sudden silence was deafening.

***

A few minutes later, I heard the click of a trunk lid.

The floor beneath me rocked. A man's voice behind me said, "Get him out. If he resists, break one of his fingers."

A pair of strong hands grabbed me by the upper arms and pulled. The sudden pressure on my numb limbs jabbed me like a hundred knife points, and I gasped. The arms kept up the pressure, pulling me back and lifting me until I was sitting upright. A different pair of hands grabbed my ankles and lifted, and I was taken out of the trunk and made to stand. I heard a snap down near my ankles, and suddenly my legs were free. I tried to stand on my own and nearly collapsed, but the man holding my upper arms prevented me from doing so.

I heard a quick scuffle behind me. Then a gasp, followed by a shriek. Erin yelled, "Let go of me, you creep!"

"She's just acting," Mike said, her voice very close. "One of them just helped her out of the van, and now she's standing off to the side, watching the guy holding you up."

"Don't!" Erin said, gasping. "You'd *better* not manhandle me like that. My uncle won't like it one bit! He knows a bunch of important people, asshole!"

"Fuck your uncle," said someone behind me.

"The guy with her is watching you," Mike said. "She's smiling at him. With his blond hair and blue eyes, he's definitely that Johnny guy you've been looking for."

I gave her a slight nod.

"Bring him inside. I'll bring the girl in with me. I've got plans for her."

"They both look like they want to have sex," Mike said flatly. "This is turning out to be both amusing and extremely disgusting. Tacky, too."

I didn't say anything as the two men holding tightly to my upper arms led me away from the vehicle.

***

I was led down a long hall.

The echoing sounds our footsteps made told me the area was still under construction. We turned and went through a doorway.

I was then led into a room. The two men stopped abruptly, turned me around and pushed me

125

into a chair. Both the seat and the back of the chair were wooden. There was no padding to absorb my weight. The force of them pushing me down played havoc on my tailbone and bound arms.

I just gritted my teeth under the hood. I didn't want to give them any excuse to get physical. So far, they hadn't been overly abusive. However, they *had* cracked me over the head, zip-tied my wrists and ankles, slipped a stupid hood over my head, and tossed me in the back of a van. In other words, they weren't exactly what you'd call stand-up dudes. But they hadn't done anything since, and I was pretty sure that crack about breaking one of my fingers was just a scare tactic. Apparently, the one speaking enjoyed reading James Bond novels. However, harsh experience told me that if I resisted in any way, I'd undoubtedly be rewarded for my efforts with a hard fist to the gut.

I decided to play their little game. So far, it didn't have the feel of something terribly dangerous. I didn't think they had any reason to kill me. Otherwise, they would have already done it. They obviously hadn't done anything drastic because they needed something from me. Since I'd always been the curious type, I found that I couldn't wait to find out what was going on.

"Stay here," one of them said.

"Don't move," the other said.

Their footsteps diminished as they left the room.

Seconds later, the door was slammed shut.

I waited to hear Mike's voice but heard only silence. I figured she was snooping around to see what she could find out from my captors. Or maybe she'd decided to explore the premises. Either way, I knew to be patient. I also knew to keep quiet just in case one of them had remained in the room and was waiting to hear me connect with my "contact."

My bound arms quickly growing numb, I sat forward and gently shrugged my shoulders to get the blood flowing in them. After about a minute, some unpleasant tingling registering in them made me grit my teeth. I waited for the pain to subside before moving them again. More tingling. Then more numbness.

Sighing, I carefully leaned back in the chair and struggled to relax. And force my mind off the pain.

Chapter 17

About five minutes later, the sudden squeal of an opening door made my pulse pound.

Two sets of footsteps came in quickly. The door closed sharply. The footsteps continued approaching and stopped just a few feet from my chair.

"It's that Johnny guy." Mike had returned and stood close beside me. "One of his friends is right behind him. His friend is finishing a roast beef sandwich. Neither of them appear to be particularly threatening. The Johnny guy is watching you and fixing the knot on his tie. He just winked and smiled at his friend."

I grinned beneath the hood.

"Know why you're here?" Grayson took one step closer to where I sat.

I nodded.

"Tell me, then."

"Tell you what?"

A sigh. "Why are you here?"

"I'm here because some asshole hit me over the head, dumped me in the back of a van, and brought me here. Otherwise, I'd be somewhere else, wouldn't I?"

A pause.

"They're looking at one another," Mike said. "They both look surprised."

"Wise guy, huh?" Grayson said.

"You asked," I replied.

His deep sigh sounded exaggerated. "What I *meant* was, do you know *why* you're here right now?"

"I just told you."

A groan. "You're some kind of trouble, you know."

"I get that a lot."

"And you're no spring chicken—"

"I figured that one out on my own, thanks. The crow's feet and the tendency to nod off after breakfast kind of gave it away. And when they quit carding me in bars, I looked at that as what some might call another clue."

"I wasn't finished."

"Sorry. Do go on."

"I started to say that you're not exactly a kid and you're definitely not a big, strong guy, but you've really got some serious moves."

"How's that?"

"Anyone your age who can take out three armed men has got to have some first-class moves."

"My biorhythm was probably on the upswing when all that happened," I said.

"Funny," Grayson said flatly.

"I tend to get a tad dangerous and slightly reckless when my life is threatened. Some might call it an adrenaline rush."

"Listen to me, Deacon. I really don't have time for this bullshit."

129

"You're the one who brought me here. You're also the one who started this ridiculous conversation. Otherwise, I'd be back in my apartment, kicking back a glass of Jack and watching *Law & Order*," or maybe HGTV."

"Now you're pissing me off. You really don't want to piss me off."

"He's angry," Mike said. "But I think he's more frightened than he's letting on."

"Why don't you just tell me why I'm here," I said. "It might save the both of us a lot of unnecessary aggravation. Besides, I've never been comfortable talking with a hood over my head. It kind of restricts my air intake—if you get what I mean. Breathing's important—especially when you need to talk."

"You do understand why I haven't taken it off, right?"

"I think so. But tell me anyway. Just to make sure we're both on the same page."

"I take it off, you see our faces. You see our faces, you're SOL. Which means we have to kill you."

"I think I get it."

"So…we're on the right page, then?"

"Maybe."

"You're thinking of something else?"

"Could be." I was thinking that if he knew a spirit was standing beside me who already told me who he was and what was going on, he'd lose his nut altogether. "But it's not really that important, is it?"

130

Another pause.

"They're looking at one another again," Mike said. "This time, they both look serious."

"It's like this," Grayson said. "We're about to make a trade."

"What sort of trade?"

"You've got something I want, and I've got something you want."

"Let's cut to the chase. What the hell could you have that I'd want?"

"Your freedom, for want of a better phrase?"

"My freedom? Seriously?"

"Do I sound like I'm joking?"

"You're saying *that's* why you conked me on the skull, tossed me in the back of a van, and brought here? To tell me something you could have told me on the phone?"

"I'm getting to it, dammit. And stop being a smartass. First of all, as you already know, I've got both you and Miss Dobbs. Also, as you already know, she has an uncle in the Police Department who has access to something I want and need. You, on the flip side, have something I have and something you need."

"Why don't you just tell me what the hell this is all about before I accidentally drift off and really piss you off?"

"All right. I'll make this easy. An extremely wealthy employer of mine needs something from the Evidence Locker at Police Headquarters. A simple trade, in this case, will be advantageous for both of us. You simply acquire what my employer

131

needs, and I set Miss Dobbs free. And, most importantly, you'll have no more trouble from us."

"That does sound simple."

"I'm glad we both think so."

"There are just two problems I can see."

"Problems?"

"Yes. Two of them."

"Go on."

"One is very obvious. What makes you think Erin's uncle will agree to let me have whatever your employer wants?"

"You two are friends, right?"

"So?"

"Friends do one another favors all the time."

"This wouldn't be a favor. It would be something that would lead to the man's prosecution, dismissal, all sorts of hefty fines, serious jail time, and life on the street as a homeless dude if and when he does get out again."

"Maybe. But believe me, this is necessary. And it really wouldn't be much of a problem. The way I hear it, Miss Dobbs' uncle is very attached to her, and is very family minded. I honestly don't think he'd do anything to jeopardize his niece's safety by getting stubborn about some piece of evidence that doesn't even involve him. You agree, don't you?"

I saw no reason to argue with him about something so obvious. "I guess you could be right."

"By the way, what was that second problem you mentioned?"

"This problem, as I see it, is also very simple, so I'll put it in simple terms. What'll make me want to do this?"

Grayson laughed. "The answer to that, my friend, is also very simple. In a nutshell, this transaction is necessary for Miss Dobbs' personal safety."

"How's that?"

"To be brief, you do this little errand and Miss Dobbs stays healthy. You don't? Well, I guess I'll leave that to your imagination."

"He's bluffing," Mike said. "This whole thing's a bluff."

I nodded but didn't say anything.

"No smartass replies this time, Mr. Deacon? Just a nod?"

"I really don't know what to say about that one."

"Does this mean you're considering working with us?"

"Not really…"

A pause. "What the hell does it mean, then?"

"Don't rush me. I'm thinking about the pros and cons."

"Pros and cons?"

"For instance, what makes you think I even care about the girl in the first place?"

Silence.

"And even if I did, what makes you think—"

"Tell Lou to break the little finger on Miss Dobbs' left hand."

133

I heard someone pressing buttons. Then the other voice, coming from just a couple of feet on Grayson's left, said softly, "Let her have it."

Moments later, a bloodcurdling scream came through the cell phone.

Alarmed by the sudden shriek, I jumped in my chair. She certainly sounded convincing enough. It made me wonder what was really going on. Grayson didn't sound like your average goon or mobster. He sounded like a car salesman with big ideas. And judging by what Mike had already told me, Grayson was bluffing his way through this. No doubt doing it to get a serious bit of work done for a friend or associate.

"She's faking it," Mike said a moment later. "She's sitting with another one of them in a room upstairs, and they're both having soda and some chicken sandwiches from Wendy's. She's also on her cell with her friend Helena. They were discussing the last episode of *Claws*. When it was time for her performance, the guy with her held his phone in front of her face. She swallowed some soda, opened her mouth wide and screamed. It was all very well done. But frightening. Anyone who can scream on cue needs therapy."

"Well?" Grayson's face was very close to mine. "Are you going to comply? Or do I have to break another one of her fingers?"

I sighed. I was getting tired of all this. My arms were totally numb, and my shoulders felt as though someone had applied a hot poker to both of them. "You really got me with that one."

"What does that mean?"

"I guess it means I'll have to do what you want."

"You don't sound convincing enough."

"You want me to get on my knees? Sorry, I don't work that way. Even if I did, I couldn't do it with my hands tied behind me and my numb shoulders, and this stupid hood over my head. I might trip or stumble on the way down. Then you'd have to get me to a hospital fast because I'm no longer a spring chicken, as you just said. And as everyone knows, old guys have brittle bones."

I heard a soft snicker from the other guy.

A moment later, a heavy set of footsteps moved in my direction. A hand pressed snugly against the back of my head. At the same time, another hand pressed against my face.

Something minty and sweet-smelling made me instantly sleepy.

Chapter 18

When I awoke, I realized that I was lying in the back seat of the Charger.

I guessed that Grayson and his thugs had given me chloroform. Holding the soaked rag snugly against the hood in front of my face made it work quickly.

As a result, I now felt groggy and nauseous. I struggled to sit up, grabbing the neck rest of the passenger seat to help me upright. Once my equilibrium took hold, my stomach began protesting. I elbowed the door open and, still gripping the neck rest, bent over and stuck my head outside. The nausea had subsided a little. Since I hadn't had much to eat earlier, I had very little to contribute to the cracked pavement below.

Still holding onto the neck rest, I raised my head a little. Bright, blurred headlights from two lanes of traffic roared by, creating a heavy miasma of exhaust fumes brushing my face. I lowered my head and breathed through my mouth until the wave dissipated.

Judging by the charcoal sky, I figured it was late at night or very early in the morning. I vaguely remembered it being close to nine o'clock when I brought Erin to the Awful Waffle. However, it now seemed an eternity since I woke up in the van.

After taking a few deep breaths, I raised my head and scanned my surroundings. My captors had obviously moved the Charger away from its spot facing the Awful Waffle. I was now sitting in a space facing the highway, about a hundred feet from the eatery. Nice of them. They obviously didn't want any of the nighttime customers watching me recover as they ate. I was actually kind of glad. I couldn't imagine trying to enjoy a meal of scrambled eggs and pancakes with some asshole outside the window, heaving his guts.

I squinted at the digital clock on the dash. It said 3:28. More than six hours since Grayson and his gang of thugs suckered me.

I stayed in that same position for few minutes, waiting for the nausea to subside. Then I sat back, leaned against the neck rest, closed my eyes and willed the grogginess and nausea to diminish.

"You know you're getting much too old for this," Mike said, close beside me.

I took another deep breath. Kept my eyes closed. Tried not to take offense. Mike was my friend. She said some things that hurt, but she only said them because she was concerned for my health and safety. But the words still hurt.

"Thanks for the vote of confidence."

"It has nothing to do with confidence. It has everything to do with your body."

"My body's in good shape for my age."

"That's the key word, isn't it?"

"Which word is that? Body? Good? Shape?"

"*Age*, you silly, silly man."

137

She had a point, but I was in no mood to continue this conversation. I had a case to finish. And to finish it, I had to hurry up and feel better. I had things to do, more people to annoy. The main thing, of course, was to call Neil and tell him what was going on.

"Nothing to say?"

"Not right now."

Her form was hazy, but I could still see her nodding. "I was right. You're not the same Ralph Deacon I've known and loved all these years."

"I'm the same. Just a little older and slightly more beat-up."

"The last time this happened, you were several years younger."

"I vaguely remember."

"It knocked you for a loop even back then."

"Yep. That memory's there, too."

"You're older now."

"I'm really glad I've got you around to keep my age issue current."

"I only bring this up because I love you and I'm worried about you."

"I love you, too."

"Thank you. The next time I bring this up, I truly hope you'll remember this conversation."

"I will."

"Really?"

"I'll try."

"Good. Because—"

"I get it, okay?"

"I'm *so* glad."

"So now that we've got *that* straightened out…"

"I'm just glad that the hoodlums we're dealing with are amateurs."

"You and me both."

"And they have no idea what they're doing."

"Right again."

"But at least they were smart enough to realize that hurting you wouldn't get them what they want."

"I'm really glad of that."

"Okay, so what's next? Your rude police buddy needs to know what's going on, right?"

"Exactly. I've got to tell him about this as quickly as possible."

"That means a phone call, doesn't it?"

"Mike, don't ever let anyone think you're dumb."

"I'll remember that."

"Because you're very bright."

"I know that, too. Know what else I know?"

"What's that?"

"Your phone and gun are in your glovebox."

My eyes shot open. Had I heard her correctly? Ignoring the throbbing in my head, I sat up and gawked at her. "Are you serious? They left my gun and phone *here*? In this *car*?"

"I honestly wouldn't joke about something like that."

"But how do you know for sure?"

"I was right here when they put you in the back seat, silly. I saw them do it."

"Sorry. I guess I should have known."

"Yes. You really should have. Now make your call."

Taking a deep breath, I carefully got out and closed the door. Then, as I leaned against the side of the car, I pulled open the passenger door. After taking my time getting back in without bumping anything important, I reached over and flipped open the glove box.

There they were, lying right there on top of the paperwork in the glovebox.

"Damn. I would have never thought…"

"Considerate, weren't they?"

"True, honest, upstanding gentlemen."

"Don't go overboard, now."

"I was being funny."

"Really?"

I ignored Mike's smug expression as I pressed the button for Neil's number.

***

After downing four cups of hot black coffee with some eggs and toast at the Awful Waffle, I began feeling a lot better.

It was now 5:00. I'd told Neil to give me some time to collect myself. Luckily for me, he told me he was more than okay with that. But even so, I knew what had to be done and that I didn't have much time to do it. Mike had kept me pretty well informed about what was going on back at the Kissimmee hotel, so I knew I couldn't trust any of them. Most of all, I knew I couldn't trust Erin, who, I sadly realized, could very well be the brains of this entire operation.

But I knew better than voice my opinion to Neil. I just told him that Erin was all right for now and that whoever had taken her told me that she would be returned unharmed the moment a certain piece of police evidence was released from Evidence.

Feeling much better, I paid for my meal and got back in the Charger with Mike. Due to the early hour, traffic wasn't heavy, and we reached the Police Station a little before 5:30 A.M.

Neil was pacing in his office when Mike and I walked in. I could tell by his unkempt appearance— and also by the unkempt appearance of the couch in his office—that he'd spent the night here.

Without a word, I staggered right over to the chair facing his desk and collapsed in it.

"Ya look like shit warmed over," he said with a scowl.

"He gets ruder each time I see him," Mike said flatly.

"I'd have to feel a hundred percent better to look that good," I told Neil.

He stopped moving and studied my expression. "What'd they do to ya?"

"Not much. Just a crack on the back of the skull and a slightly bumpy ride in a van with a hood pulled over my head. It was the chloroform that really did me in later on, once they'd finished telling me their demands."

Still watching me closely, he sat down. He actually looked worried. I would have been touched if I hadn't felt like collapsing at any second. "You

141

okay now? I mean, ya good to go? Or do I have to get ya checked out by one of our—"

"I'm fine. I just had a big breakfast. I'll be good as new in an hour or so." I rubbed my eyes. "Did you find those three I left for you?"

He shook his head. "I sent Benton and a uniform, but there was no sign of anyone. They were either picked up, or skedaddled on their own. We did find the two pieces ya left in the bushes, though."

I figured the one driving the car probably got to the first two right after I'd left. The one I suckered in the Charger later on I wasn't sure about, but I was much too tired to think of that right now.

"Okay, then." Neil was obviously ready for some answers. "Let's go through this, step by step."

"Well, as I said on the phone, Erin's definitely sleeping with the wrong crowd."

"You sure it's Grayson?"

"I got a glimpse of him just before they hit me on the back of the skull and jammed the hood over my head." I decided to fudge a little on the details. Otherwise, he'd be grilling me the rest of the day.

"And they want something from the Evidence Locker?"

"That's about it, in a nutshell."

Neil sat back and stared at the ceiling. I could tell this was killing him. He didn't deserve this crap at all. It concerned his niece, who he probably held in his arms when she was just an infant and might have even fed her the bottle and rocked her to sleep. Something like that stuck with a guy. I had no idea

142

what he was going to tell his sister about this, but whatever it was, she wouldn't like it. Not one bit.

After a while, he snapped out of it and gazed at me. "You're sure she's in on this? I mean really totally sure?"

I decided to make this as easy for him as possible. "I kind of think she cares a lot for the guy. At that age, females fall really easily. But I'd guess that he sold her a bill of goods. Since he's at least ten years older than she is, he knows how easy it is to get a good firm grip on a young female. All he has to do is impress her and make her feel special— which is surprisingly easy for guys in their mid- to late thirties. If she's smitten, which she clearly is, she'll do whatever he says."

"But she's bright, Deacon..." Neil's face suggested both fear and frustration. "Mature. More focused than most of her friends. And she knows what's going on. She definitely knows what it means to mess with key evidence."

"You told her not to bring her cell phone, didn't you?"

"I thought we already discussed--" He gawked at me. "Are you saying what I *think* you're saying?"

"How do you suppose they found us?"

"I specifically told her about the cell...and that stupid iPad."

"Well, when you see her again, be prepared."

"For what?"

"I trashed the phone, the iPad, and her laptop."

His eyes filled the sockets. "She brought along the damn laptop *as well*?"

143

I nodded.

Neil jumped up from his chair and paced nearly a minute in silence. Then he stopped, went back to his chair, and collapsed in it. "I honestly don't know about this…" He shook his head. "Why would she even consider something doing like this? She knows how seriously I take this job…"

"Maybe Grayson didn't tell her what he planned to do. Or maybe he lied to her and told her something that didn't sound too bad, or illegal. For all we know, he might have told her a friend was being railroaded and that you could get him off by turning the other way and letting something slip through the boards. He might even have told her that it wouldn't get you in trouble."

Neil still had that tragic look on his face. "She'd see through something like that…wouldn't she?"

"Not if she's nuts about the guy."

Neil went silent, thinking it over. I could tell the cop in him was winning over the uncle bit. "You said she wasn't manhandled, tied up or forced in any way?"

"Yes. I did."

"You were hooded. How'd you know?"

Once again, I decided to fudge the details. "Believe it or not, there was a slight tear in the fabric of the hood. I couldn't see much, but I did see that she wasn't tied up or hooded."

Neil thought that over. I hoped he wouldn't see through it.

144

"And you're sure—I mean positive—no one's hurt her?"

I nodded.

Neil got up and started pacing again. "This really and truly sucks. Big-time. I mean *sucks*."

"I know. And I have no idea what we should do."

"We were all good to her. Let her have whatever she wanted. Treated her with respect. What the hell happened?"

"Life."

"Yeah. It always comes down to that, doesn't it?"

"It has to."

"We can't keep them trapped in a bubble until they're adults, can we?"

I didn't reply.

He stopped pacing and gawked at me. "If that asshole Grayson's really pulling her strings, he'll want this to go down the way he's been told."

"Exactly."

"But what if…what if something goes wrong?"

"If he screws up, I honestly don't know what he'll do."

"We still don't know if Grayson's on Vega's payroll."

"Something tells me he isn't."

"How can ya tell?"

I thought of what Mike had told me about the others but knew I couldn't very well tell Neil. He just wouldn't be able to accept hearsay from a spirit.

Once again, I decided to play it by ear. "Just a guess."

"You could be wrong."

"I know. I just don't think I am."

"Trusting that gut of yours again?"

"That, plus the fact that I kind of think Vega's men would have been much rougher on both of us."

"Even though Erin might be involved?"

"Vega doesn't care about Anglos. Especially Anglo females. He's an old-fashioned Hispanic who thinks women were put on earth to serve men. You know as well as I do how the average American woman would piss off a man like Vega."

Neil nodded but remained silent.

"I've got something else that I've been kicking around up there," I said. "Care to hear it?"

"Toss it over."

"That third guy I suckered? The one at the motel on Aloma?"

"What about it?"

"He was definitely Hispanic."

Neil frowned. "One of Vega's?"

"Could very well be. Aloma isn't anywhere near Kissimmee, but you never can tell with these mob guys anymore. They go where they're needed."

Neil took a deep breath. "Know what this means?"

"I know what it *could* mean…"

"Spill it."

"One of Grayson's men could be working with someone else."

"Someone other than Vega?"

"Or against."

"You're serious?"

I shrugged. "Stranger things have happened."

"If you're right, this thing...could explode...at any second."

"I hope I'm wrong, but..."

"I know." Neil's expression was grim. "We've got to sincerely hope you're *totally* wrong. Because if you're right..."

"I know. This could be it for Erin."

Chapter 19

Neil took a bottle of Scotch and two glasses out of his bottom drawer and poured about an inch into each.

He handed me a glass. I took it gratefully and had a belt. Even though it was early in the morning, and I didn't care much for Scotch, it was damned good single malt stuff and went down smoothly. Besides, I needed a strong drink right now and didn't want to quibble.

Neil opened another drawer. He took out my cell and put it on his desktop. A second later, it buzzed.

"How'd you do that?" I asked.

He had another sip of Scotch. "Magic." Then he gestured. "Go 'head. Answer it. It might be those assholes."

I picked it up. The display said, *UNKNOWN CALLER*. "Morning, whoever this is…"

"Deacon?"

"That's me," I said rather cheerfully. I knew it was Grayson and didn't want him to think I was hurting over my experience with him and his third-class clowns. "How goes it?"

"Still the smartass, I see."

Neil shrugged. He obviously wanted to know who was calling.

I mouthed the name Grayson. Then I said, "You're one of the guys who put out my lights twice in one night, right?"

"Yeah, still the smartass."

Neil put down his glass and pushed his chair forward. Then he picked up his pen and wrote something down on his pad. He pushed it across the desk. It said: *Erin OK?* He picked up his cell, got up and went over to the door to whisper to someone, no doubt to tell them to trace the call.

To Grayson, I said, "Is that why you called? To see that I hadn't changed my attitude about life in general in just a couple of hours? By the way, thanks for the chloroform. I needed the shuteye."

"Ram it, Deacon. I didn't call to hear any more of your bullshit."

"Well, you ought to know by our brief talk that bullshit and I happen to be one with each other. A packaged set. We've been buds most of my life. It gets even worse, sometimes, and the bullshit actually takes over in times of stress. Especially when I'm forcibly taken somewhere and I'm not even able to enjoy my new surroundings."

Neil came right back and sat down. He lightly tapped his blotter with his knuckles. Giving me the sign to get to the point.

"Once again, Deacon, shut up."

"All right. Out of respect for Erin, I will. By the way, how is she?"

"She's fine. For now."

I gave Neil the OK sign. He sat back and seemed to relax.

"I take it you're with her uncle right now."

"How'd you know?"

"I've got my ways. I hope you're not tracing this call."

"Wouldn't think of it. Friends don't do that to one another, do they? Oh, wait. You're not a friend, are you? Friends don't kidnap one another, tie them up and shove a hood over their head."

"You finished with your bullshit yet?"

"If this means you're about to tell me why you're calling, then yeah. I am. Otherwise, nope. I've still got a way to go."

"This won't take long. Give the phone to her uncle. I've got a locker number he needs to find for me."

"You want that to happen now?"

"Dammit, Deacon…"

I handed Neil his cell. Neil took it and held it to his ear. He took a breath. "Haversack…" He grabbed his pen again and began scribbling. "Yeah. Got it. You wouldn't by any chance let me talk to my—"

He winced and pulled the cell away from his ear. "Niece," he said, putting it down on the blotter. "I didn't think so. Asshole."

"Have any idea what it is?" I asked.

He was studying what he'd written down. "I can tell by the prefix where it's located in the locker. Other than that? Not a clue." He picked up his office phone. "There's one easy way to find out, though." He began dialing.

***

150

Fifteen minutes later, after making three separate calls, Neil put down the receiver, sighed tiredly and shook his head.

"What is it?" I asked.

"Something just doesn't figure here. This evidence seems to hinge on an audio message that was used in a case last year, involving a stash house that led us to one of Vega's top men. The audio was taken from a cell phone that had been used in a drop-off."

"What happened with the case?"

"Mistrial. It's rescheduled for another go about three months from now."

"Names mentioned?"

"Vega, of course, but only as Paseo."

"That's the name Vega uses for his businesses."

"The others were Stefan Torres and someone whose voice was virtually unrecognizable. From what I was told by the investigating officers, the voice could belong to a Robert Galvani."

"I didn't think Vega used Italians."

"He doesn't."

"Then what's this all about?"

"The time factor. Someone's obviously trying to buy for time to doctor the audio or make it unusable for the retrial. This is beginning to stink, big-time."

"Don't tell me Galvani is from the Raguzzo Mob."

"That's exactly what I'm thinking."

"What else are you thinking? The same thing that's going on in my head?"

151

"That one's easy. Maybe too easy. Galvani running a scam on Raguzzo? And, to top it all off, a couple of Vega's men running the same scam on Vega? With that idiot Grayson involved as well? As a go-between?"

"That's basically what I'm thinking, too."

"Grayson found out about Erin, possibly through Galvani or someone else, and decided to pull the oldest trick in the book to get her involved in this."

"And Grayson benefits by pulling her into this and then getting you involved."

Neither of us said anything.

Mike was the one who spoke first. "This is bad, isn't it?"

"This is *very* bad," I said for her benefit.

Neil nodded. "Someone wants me to sneak that audio out of evidence and hand it over to the folks who've got my niece's life at stake. This is too damned obvious."

"But it sounds about right," I said.

"And the longer this plays out, the easier it'll be for Vega to find out about it and bully his way into it. And ya know what'll happen when he does."

"I don't want to think about that."

"Neither do I."

"I just hope the bastard hasn't gotten wind of it yet."

Neil didn't reply. I could tell by his miserable expression what he was thinking.

"What I don't understand is why Grayson's involved in the first place," I said. "He's definitely small-time. Hot cars, maybe some drug trafficking. A punk like him wouldn't want to go against someone like Vega."

"C'mon, Deacon. This one's obvious, too. Grayson's no doubt dirtier than we're giving him credit for. And since he deals in hot cars in the Kissimmee area, he probably also deals with Vega."

"And your niece? She's pretty, bright, and has the chance to make something of herself."

He shrugged. "As we've both already decided, she fell for his flash."

"Well, right now, she doesn't seem to be in any danger."

"But what about later?" Neil immediately put on his frightened expression. "What happens when I tell this asshole I can't possibly deliver the piece of evidence they want in exchange for her life?"

Chapter 20

Before we left Neil's office, he opened his desk drawer, pulled out another disposable phone, and handed it to me.

"What's this?" I asked.

"There's a three-minute message on it. It's pretty garbled, but it just might do exactly what we hope it'll do."

"What's that?"

"Give us a little extra time."

I tried imagining what he was trying to tell me, but it just didn't make sense. "You're sure about this?"

"No. But it's the best thing I could come up with for now."

Twenty minutes later, Mike and I sat in the TransAm in the rear lot of the Police Station. It was just before seven, and the lot had already been showing steady morning activity.

"I've never seen your rude police buddy so depressed," Mike said. "I actually feel sorry for him."

"He's very close to Erin. It pisses me off that she fell for Grayson and has been letting him manipulate her like that. It's gonna take Neil some serious money to get her off the hook and keep her out of trouble. The family will need to find her a top-notch attorney, and they'll ask Neil to get them one. She's already facing several felonies."

"I'm not so sure she's thinking of that right now," Mike said.

"I guess she's too smitten for anything like that."

Mike nodded.

"I just can't see it. Erin's bright. She might not be on her own just yet, but she's smart enough to know what's going on. And that there are bad guys out there who don't look like—or even act like—bad guys."

"It's easy to be manipulated when you're a young girl."

I stared at Mike's hazy image and tried to imagine what she was thinking. As usual, her large almond eyes said it all. "It happened to you, too?" I asked.

"It happens to all of us."

"It's that easy?"

"That's really not the issue."

"What *is*?"

"A girl longs to be appreciated. It's a daddy thing, when it comes right down to it. A little girl needs to be loved and cherished by her father. In the accepted scenario, everything she does is a good thing. When she's just a child, he puts her in his lap and reads her fairy tales and tells her all sorts of romantic stories about a white knight that will come into her life one day and take her away to live in a big, beautiful castle with him. She believes him because she's his princess, and her daddy would never lie to her. She knows he will always be there when he needs her."

"What about the other scenario? Reality, in other words?"

"That's entirely different. And also very sad. In this case, the father is not a very nice man. He's either much too busy with his business, or he doesn't care much at all about being a father. Or, even worse, he actually hates being a father in the first place. He ignores her or belittles her whenever the opportunity arises. The daughter, of course, is heartbroken, but she never gives up, and constantly bends over backward to please him. But she never does. As a result, she spends the rest of her life going after the wrong men just so she can feel better about herself. She figures any attention she gets is worth the effort, but it never really is because she has no self-esteem, and no inner sense of knowing a good man when she sees one."

"I don't know anything about Erin's father. I imagine that he's probably an okay guy. Neil would've told me, otherwise."

"From what you've said, her mother cares about her. That's not the same as her father's love, but at least she's got her mother on her side. And of course, her uncle."

"You never told me anything about your father, did you?"

"Water over the bridge now."

I could tell by her somewhat cold expression that it was time to move on. "From what Neil told me, Erin hasn't been neglected at all. So, from what

156

you've just said, she shouldn't be looking for a daddy substitute at all."

"It doesn't matter. Not when she's got someone like Grayson in her life who's giving her all this attention. For a girl, attention from the opposite sex is just about everything."

"He's using her."

"As I just said, it doesn't matter. When the attention's there..." She shrugged.

"Don't forget the bad-boy thing."

"Unfortunately, that's an added incentive."

I took the disposable cell phone Neil gave me and stared at it. Hopefully, Neil's new tactic wouldn't get Erin killed.

"I don't know if that's going to work at all." Mike was obviously feeling the same way.

"I don't know, either. But Neil couldn't very well sign in to the Evidence Locker and remove something that would let several guilty men walk on a bunch of major felonies and endanger his own career in the process."

"So he hands you a cell phone with some garbled voices on it instead?"

"As he told me, to give us some time."

"How much time will it take them to take it from you, switch it on and find out they don't have what they want?"

"I'm hoping at least ten seconds or so."

"Then?"

"Then they'll probably do something really bad to Erin. And probably me, as well."

"So what sort of other bargaining chip do we have?"

"Just you."

***

Grayson called me on my cell precisely at 9:00.

"You have the evidence?" he asked.

"I've got it in my hot little hands. Actually, I've got it in my jacket pocket." I patted it. "Yep, it's right here."

"Good boy. Now listen carefully. And don't try tracing this. For one thing, the phone's a burner. For another, you'll just piss me off."

"I certainly don't want to do *that*, do I?"

"No. You really don't."

"But don't worry. I honestly don't care. I just want this bullshit over with."

"We're on the same page, then. Just remember this. You'll be all right as long as you follow orders."

"How about Erin?"

"The same goes for her. But if you deviate in any way from the instructions I'm about to give you—"

"Cut the crap." I was getting tired of all this and wanted it to be over. "I know all about the threats, okay? I don't do this, Erin dies. I don't do that, Erin dies. I do this, Erin dies. Save yourself some valuable time and just give me the damned directions."

A pause. "Wow... Testy, ain't we?"

"I've got reason to be. I've got a nice, comfortable, air-conditioned apartment with a soft

158

sofa in my living room waiting to accommodate my tired butt, a full bottle of Jack Daniels waiting for me to slowly drain it, and a widescreen waiting for me to turn it on and watch it. Life will be good once I stop dealing with you idiots and get back home. Now let's get this crap over with, all right?"

"Deacon, you want to know something?"

"I already know. I'm an asshole. I've known that for a long time. Now what do I do? Where do I go? And when do I get there?"

"All right. Here's your instructions. Got something to write this all down?"

I got a small pad and pen from my console. "I'm ready."

"First of all, you need to get on the Trail and head south. Go all the way to One-Ninety-Two. Get on One-Ninety-Two and head west. About two and a half miles later, make a left onto Armstrong and go south. Drive past Grissom. But don't go too far. Once you pass Grissom, you'll see another turnoff that goes east. This one will take you to a line of warehouses. Drive over to the last one on the right, at the far end. Park in front of the door and you'll receive further instructions. But the turnoff isn't far from Grissom. If you've reached Commerce, you've gone too far."

"That's it?"

"That's it."

"Once I park where I'm supposed to, then what?"

"You'll receive detailed instructions by phone. In other words, don't forget your phone."

"I'm not an idiot."

"I didn't say you were. You're just a smartass. But bring the phone. You'll need it."

"What about the evidence I'll have with me?"

"As I just said—"

"I'll receive instructions from there. Yeah. I get it."

"Good. Be there at ten tonight."

"Ten? Tonight?"

"That's what I just said."

"That's thirteen hours from now."

"I'm so glad you can do simple math."

"Why not earlier?"

"You got a heavy date or something? Deacon, just do as you're told and everything'll go smoothly. Get it?"

"But—"

"One other thing. No cops. And no tail."

"Of course not."

Click.

I stared at the cell and resisted the strong urge to toss it. I gazed at Mike.

"Don't bother doing anything stupid or foolish," she said. "I heard everything."

"Why tonight rather than an hour or so from now?"

"Maybe they're watching you and want to make sure you don't do anything they don't like. Or maybe they want to wait until there's less traffic so they can keep tabs on you easier."

Mike was probably right, but I just didn't like the fact that this wouldn't end in an hour or so.

160

"Just do as they say. Otherwise, this won't end the way it's supposed to."

"You're sure Erin's in no danger?"

"So far, it looks like she's definitely got her hand in this," Mike said.

"Neil's not gonna like this. His nerves are already shot."

"Well, I don't think you've got any other choice, do you?"

"Nope. None." Sighing deeply, I punched in Neil's number.

Chapter 21

Later that night, Mike and I met Neil and Detective Miranda Benton in the side lot of a 7-Eleven on 192, a couple of miles west of South Orange Blossom Trail. I'd used my spare time to return the Charger and get back my trusty TransAm.

Neil sat in the passenger's seat of a late-model black Challenger, Benton behind the wheel. Neil drove a silver SUV, leading me to assume the Challenger was Benton's ride. Since Neil always liked being the one in charge, I decided not to ask why he wasn't driving. We had more important things to worry about.

Neil glanced at his watch as I eased the TransAm in the space next to them. "Nine-thirty-five," he said, and turned his head in the direction of the storm of passing traffic on 192. "Plenty of time. Armstrong's not even ten minutes from here."

"I'd better go inside and get some coffee," I said.

Neil had another quick peek at the traffic. "Think we're being watched? We were pretty careful once we left the Station."

"I don't want to take any chances. Grayson may not be hardcore, but he obviously knows what he's doing. I'd guess that this was planned for tonight so his guys could have the whole day to keep an eye on what we've been doing. They could very well be out there somewhere in that traffic. And don't forget, he's managed to take control of Erin without any trouble, and did it pretty well."

"I'm gonna nail that bastard, too." Neil's expression was fierce.

"We'll get him, Neil."

"I know we will."

I got out of the car, went into the brightly lit, half-deserted store and fixed a cup of black, awful-smelling coffee from one of the three coffeemakers bubbling in the back. I paid and left. The moment I got back in the TransAm, I slipped the cup into the cup holder and glanced at my watch.

"I'd better get going," I told Neil, and switched on the ignition.

"We've got someone watching your ride," Neil said. "A partner of Benton's. You won't see him, but he'll see you."

"He's really good." Benton tilted her head so I could see her. "He worked undercover for nearly five years, surveilling the cartels. He knows what he's doing."

"I'm sure he'll do just fine," I said. "But I'm not worried about that. I'm worried about what they're gonna do when they take this cell and play it."

"It's a tape of me and another cop talking," Neil said. "As I told you, it's garbled. We were discussing an open case we'd worked on a few years earlier. There are one or two similarities that could mirror this stash house case. It might just keep these morons confused for the time it takes us

163

to get all set up. As I said before, you'll give us valuable time if you drop it when you hand it over. Make sure you drop it on a hard floor, or concrete. But make it convincing."

"I can be a genuine klutz when I want to be." I put the car into reverse.

"Deacon?"

"Yeah?"

"Be careful. Find Erin but be careful. As I've told you before, I don't like paperwork. You get killed? I'll be smothered in the shit for weeks."

"Sounds horrible."

"I'm serious, now…"

"Don't worry. I promise I won't make you do any unnecessary paperwork." I backed out of the space and eased back onto the busy stretch of 192 heading west.

***

I pulled onto Armstrong at just a few minutes before 10:00.

As Grayson had said, the road I was looking for would be lined with warehouses. I counted at least eight of them as I eased down the short stretch that extended to the end. Spotlights attached to the individual roofs highlighted the front of each parking area and entrance, with orange haze spilling from the streetlights at each end, brightening both entrance and exit.

I pulled up to the entrance of the end unit and stopped.

"Kind of eerie," Mike said.

164

I scanned the lot and noticed that it was empty. "I know. Especially since I seem to be the only vehicle here."

My cell buzzed.

At that same moment, I gazed at the spot lighting the area around me and on both sides of the TransAm. Beneath it, a small black box was aimed directly at the TransAm. In its center, a tiny pinpoint of red light told me I was being monitored.

"See that?" I asked Mike.

"Looks like a camera."

"That's exactly what it is."

"Then they're watching everything you do."

"They're even more careful than I thought."

"Want me to go inside and see what's happening?"

"Good idea."

"Be right back."

As soon as she vanished, I brought the cell up to my ear. "Yeah?"

"You're early." It was Grayson.

"Want me to leave, go see a movie or something, then come right back? I hear Matt Damon just made a new one."

"You're such a funny guy, Deacon. You really need to do stand-up comedy."

"I'm told that everywhere I go."

"Why'd it take you so long to answer?"

"I was checking out my new surroundings. I'm a private detective. It's something I do all the time. It's something we all do. We like to know where everything is."

"All right, I think I got it. In other words, you spotted the camera."

"Yeah. I spotted your damned camera."

"It looked like you were talking to someone. Were you talking to someone, Deacon?"

"I talk to myself a lot. That's something else I do all the time. In my line of work, you talk to yourself. In fact—"

"All right, all right. Enough. Just shut up and do exactly as I say."

I sighed.

"Did you hear me, Deacon?"

I didn't reply.

"Deacon? You deaf? What the hell's going on?"

"You just told me to shut up."

"All right, smartass. Let's get this thing going. Get out of the damned car and walk up to the door. It's unlocked. Come in, then walk over to the desk. It'll be on your right, about ten paces from the door. Take that piece of evidence you've brought with you and put it on the desk."

Silence.

"Then what?"

"I'll let you know."

"Is that it?"

"That's it."

"Coming in…" I pocketed the cell and pushed open the door.

Mike appeared beside me. She looked frightened. "Don't go in there right now."

"Why not?"

166

"Johnny Grayson's in there."

"I think he should be. He's handling this, isn't he?"

"He was…"

The troubled look on her face frightened me. "What are you trying to tell me, Mike?"

"He's not handling this anymore."

"What?"

"He's dead."

"I just talked to him."

"He's still dead."

"Are you sure?"

Mike gave me one of her many stern expressions. "Are you serious?"

"Sorry. What was I thinking?" Something occurred to me. "Did you happen to see him when he…when he left his body?"

"Is that your way of asking me if I got to say anything to him?"

"That's pretty much it, yes."

She shook her head. "Sorry. I must have just missed his passing."

I sat back and gawked at the semi-dark aluminum building in front of me. My mind reeled as I struggled to come up with something. I couldn't just sit here. If Johnny Grayson was dead, that meant several things, none of them good. And this meant Neil wasn't about to have an enjoyable evening, either.

But the problem remained. I had to go in there.

"Any idea how he died?" I asked her.

"He's lying on his back, and his head is at an unnatural angle. Offhand, I'd say his neck was snapped. I'm no expert, but…" She shrugged.

"Yeah, that would do it, all right. Can you tell how long ago it happened?"

"Not long at all. Possibly only a moment or two after you talked to him."

"That means one of his cronies just changed the game plan."

"What are you gonna do now?"

"I don't know, but whatever I do, I've got to do it—"

My cell buzzed.

"Fast," I finished.

"I don't know how you're gonna do this," Mike said, "but you'd better call your rude police buddy as soon as possible."

"I know." I brought the phone up to my ear. "Yeah?"

"What's the holdup?" a different voice asked.

"Holdup? There's a holdup?"

"Cut the shit, asshole. Why the hell are ya still sittin' in that pile of junk?"

I caught the slight Brooklyn accident right off. However, that wasn't what I was concerned about right now. I didn't like anyone insulting my classic ride. "I'll have you know that I'm sitting in my classic TransAm as I speak."

"It's a pile of junk, asshole. Like I just said."

"First of all, it's not a pile of junk. As I just said, it's a classic car, and—"

"It's older than I am, you moron."

168

"That's what makes it a classic, dammit."

"I said, cut the shit and get your fuckin' ass in here so I can take what ya got and give ya back your bitch."

I didn't reply. I was frantically thinking of some other strategy I could use to delay this.

"Did ya hear me, asshole?"

"Why am I talking to you?" I decided I might be able to stretch this out if I found out what was going on. "What happened with Grayson? Why isn't he talking to me now?"

"He can't come to the phone right now."

"Why not?"

"Why so interested?"

"I guess I figured this was kind of important enough for him to see it through to the end."

"He had to make a call. You know…"

"You mean he's in the john?"

"Yeah. Let's go with that."

"He couldn't take his phone into the john with him? What model is it? Something that doesn't respond too well to plumbing? Or can't he do two things at one time?"

"He ain't available. Leave it at that and get your ass inside."

"I'd like to know what happened first."

"Cut the stall, dickhead. We have a deal, and—"

"My deal was with Grayson."

A pause.

"Well, now ya got *me* to deal with."

"I don't even know who the hell you are."

"You don't need to know who the hell I am, asshole. All you really need to do is shut up and do as you're told. You know what happens if ya don't, right?"

"I can imagine."

"Then shut the fuck up, get outa that pile of shit and bring that piece of evidence inside."

Click.

I ignored his last insult and pocketed the phone. "I don't have any choice, Mike. I've got to go in there and do as they say. I just hope Erin's still alive. Something tells me that the guy who just killed Grayson is the guy I was just talking to. Something also tells me that if Erin's inside, she's either dead or will soon be."

"I'll look for her the moment you step inside."

"Thanks." Now more nervous than ever, I approached the metal door. Just as I pulled it open, she vanished.

The room was very large and poorly-lit. It looked like some sort of supply room. Stacks and bundles piled on dozens of palettes in five- and six-feet heights cluttered most of the open area. The palettes had been placed two or three feet from one another, enabling anyone to walk past them to get to another area. A large opening separated with wide vertical plastic flaps faced the opposite wall, which I gathered was the entrance to the loading dock on the opposite side of the building.

A large shape lay on the concrete floor about fifteen feet behind the desk Grayson had mentioned.

In the semi-dark, it looked like some sort of sack. I suspected it was Grayson.

Enough. I had to forget about what might have happened and forced myself to focus and concentrate on the business at hand.

On the surface of the desk, a small lamp lit up the blotter. A ledger, a plastic cup containing several pens, a thick notepad and an in-box tray also took up space on the blotter.

I took Neil's cell out from the inside pocket of my jacket. As Neil had instructed, I accidentally dropped it as I was reaching over to set it on the desk. I picked it up from the floor and placed it gently on the blotter.

My cell buzzed.

I pulled it out and put it against my ear. "Now what?"

"You're an asshole, Deacon."

"Is that why you called? To tell me what everyone in Orlando already knows? Or is there something else you'd like me to know?"

"Ya think you're dealing with morons?"

"Well, since you asked—"

"You're dead, asshole. That isn't even the right phone."

"How would you know?" I turned and quickly scanned the large area. "I don't even see you—"

"*Duck*!" Mike's hysterical order sent a chill down my spine. "Right *now*!"

I dropped to the floor in front of the desk.

Four quick blasts from an automatic pistol roared just inches above my head, slamming into the metal wall twenty feet from me.

Chapter 22

Guns drawn, Neil and Benton, flanked by three armed Kissimmee police officers, slipped through the open warehouse door within minutes.

I'd managed to hide underneath the metal desk as they came in, but no other shots were fired.

"Deacon! Where the hell *are* ya?" His gun held straight out, Neil stood less than five feet from the open door. Benton, her gun also held out, stood a comfortable distance away from Neil. The three others moved cautiously amongst the palettes, their assault weapons probing every direction.

"Over here. Under the desk. I haven't been able to see if I'm still alone."

Several flashlights sprayed simultaneously in my direction.

I held up an arm to shield my eyes. "Don't blind me, now. I might have to drive home a little later and don't want to get a ticket."

"You all right?"

"I've been better, but yeah, I'll make it."

Neil came right over, bent, and held out his hand. I grabbed it. He pulled me upright while Benton spoke to her cell. The others continued searching the area. Someone found a light switch, and more than a dozen six-foot-long overhead fluorescents flickered and popped instantly, spraying the area with fluttering light. Benton slowly approached Grayson's body and said something to her phone. She turned her head in our direction. "Here, Chief."

Neil went over. He, Benton, and one uniform bent over the body.

"The shooter's gone," Mike said as I watched the activity.

"Did you happen to see him?" I whispered.

"He apparently had an escape route worked out using the loading dock. I did see a dirty gray van pulling out from Grissom and heading toward the main highway."

"A gray van?"

She nodded. "The same one they used to take you and Erin to that hotel."

"Interesting. I wonder if he went back there. I'm also wondering if Erin was in the van."

"I couldn't tell. Sorry about that."

"No problem."

"Are you sure? I really should have checked."

"You can't possibly be serious. You saved my life. Don't ever be sorry, Mike."

Neil came over. He was pocketing his cell. "They're bringing out a bus for Grayson. Any sign of Erin?"

"No. Sorry."

"What went wrong, Deacon?"

"From what I gather, it was probably just your basic power struggle, and Grayson lost."

"Obviously, but what happened with the fake cell? I can't help noticing that it's lying over there on the desk blotter."

"Whoever I was talking to apparently knew it wasn't the genuine article."

"Without even checking it out?"

I nodded. "Whoever I talked to obviously knew you didn't pay a recent visit to the Evidence Room."

Neil groaned. "I'll bet I know damn well what else you're gonna say..."

"Whoever planned all this has got a buddy."

"And this bastard obviously works at the Station."

***

After the M.E. and the EMT guys arrived, I got back in the TransAm to get out of their way. And, of course, to think of something.

"We've got to find her," Mike said, sitting beside me.

"I know. And we've got to do it before the guy who killed Grayson decides to get rid of Erin. Now that he knows he's not getting that audio, he's gonna be desperate. I don't know who he's dealing with exactly, but I'll wager that a couple of Vega's men are involved, and that would make anyone scared to death. Especially when they've been working a scam job on the big man and it went sour."

"I can lead you to the hotel, you know."

"What makes you think he's there?"

"Well, he'd feel safe there, wouldn't he? Especially since he thinks no one else knows he's there. No one except for the Grayson guy. And he's dead."

"And, of course, Erin."

"Of course. And since he thinks he's safe, he might not be in so much of a hurry to do what he's planning to do with her. He might even take his time. Which is what we really need him to do."

"That's right. The one thing he doesn't know is the thing that's going to bring him down."

"What's that?"

"You."

"If you don't mind, I prefer not being referred to as a thing. Bargaining chip was insulting enough."

"Uh, sorry, Mike."

"But you're right. He has no idea anyone knows where he is."

"No one alive, that is."

Neil came over. He looked even more exhausted and frustrated than he was before.

"Find anything in there?" I asked.

"Benton made some calls. This place is being rented by some out-of-state developer no one seems to know anything about. Benton asked a friend of hers to hack into the FBI databanks and try to track it down, but there's nothing. All we seem to know is that it's been rented out for two months, but there's been no recent activity."

"What about all those palettes cluttering up the place?"

"Judging by the stamps on them, they've been sitting there for three months."

"What are they, exactly?"

"Building supplies. Home Depot used this unit for their Kissimmee branch. Apparently, they left some of their stuff here once management changed hands."

"Terrific. We know absolutely nothing, then."

"Seems that way."

"I wonder what they were planning."

"I'm wondering who *they* are," Neil said with a scowl.

"From what I gathered, the guy I was talking to, the gentleman who no doubt broke Grayson's neck, sounded northern. I detected a slight Brooklyn accent."

"Think it was Galvani?"

"Your guess is as good as mine. Since Raguzzo is originally from New York City, many of his guys have come down from that same area. This might tell us that it could be someone working with Papa Joe. Or moonlighting with someone moonlighting behind Vega's back. This could be a future drug drop, for all we know. Any idea how much the rent is?"

"No idea. But these guys don't seem to care about such tiny details. They handle more jack in one night than most of us see in a lifetime."

"Well, I definitely have to find out what we're dealing with." I switched on the ignition.

"You actually have a plan in the works?"

"I might."

"Wanna share?"

"I'm not really sure about—"

177

"Deacon, this is my niece we're talking about…"

"That's exactly why I don't want to do anything that might get her hurt, or worse."

"If you've got some idea where this asshole went…"

"Just a hunch."

"I'm going with you."

"You can't, Neil."

"Why not?"

"Because I'm not sure what I'll find."

"Deacon…" Neil was obviously both angry and frustrated.

I just sighed.

"It's his niece," Mike said.

I gave her a quick look of worry.

"We can still do this," she said. "He might even be useful. It'll be tricky, but we can swing it."

I decided Mike could be right. Anyway, the more I thought about it, the more I realized Neil should be involved. Besides, he was an experienced, seasoned cop. He was armed, and he was also a crack shot.

"All right. As long as you let me do this my way."

"I gotta be there if and when ya find her."

"One last time, Neil. My way?"

He stood there in silence. I could tell this was difficult for him. I could also tell he trusted me. After a deep sigh, he finally nodded. "Your way, then."

***

178

Ten minutes later, as I headed west on 192, Neil asked, "Are ya gonna tell me what you're doing?" When I didn't reply, he asked, "How the hell do ya know where we're going? Or, more appropriately, why we're going there?"

"A hunch." I glanced at the rearview, which reflected Mike's image in the seat behind me. She was giving me one of her wry smiles.

"A *hunch*?" Neil was looking at me as if I'd just told him I could fly like a bird. "You're wasting all this time—and my niece's *life*—on a damn *hunch*?"

"A *strong* hunch."

Neil continued glaring. I could tell this wasn't sitting well with him. After all, he was a cop. A facts-and-figures guy who routinely considered hunches but didn't take much stock in them when there were very few facts to back them up. And since this hunch of mine involved his niece, he was treating it with a lot of suspicion. "Even so, Deacon, you actually wanna rely on a strong *hunch* with my niece's life on the line? How can you be sure this *hunch* of yours'll even hold water? How can ya be sure—"

"Actually, it's a strong, solid, granite-hard, ears-ringing, nerve-twitching, gut-bending hunch." I forced myself to forget the idea of stopping at the next intersection and kicking the man out onto the curb.

Neil sat back and sighed heavily. He began watching the closed businesses and vacant parking lots we passed. I could tell he was trying to accept my way of doing things but was having a rough time. I couldn't blame him. A hard-nosed cop like him always stuck to the facts—especially when the life of a loved one was at stake.

But I couldn't very well tell him that my hunch depended on a beautiful dead lady who had been working with me and helping me solve most of my cases for the last ten years. A lovely spirit who'd saved my life more than a dozen times. A spirit who could do incredible things.

"He's just worried," Mike said.

I nodded.

"We'll find her," she added.

"We'll find her," I told Neil. "I promise."

He shot his glaring face back in my direction. "How the hell can you promise me something like *that*? You got *any* idea where she is? I mean really? Besides your strong, solid, granite-hard, ears-ringing *hunch*?"

"Yeah. As a matter of fact, I do."

"But you won't tell me anything else about it."

"I'd rather not till the times comes."

"And when the hell will *that* time be?"

"When I'm absolutely certain my strong, solid, granite-hard, ears-ringing hunch turns out to be right on the money."

Chapter 23

Twenty minutes and five intersections later, Mike said, "Turn left here."

I did as she said, and we went down a winding narrow dirt road past a fairly new subdivision on the left and another smaller, newer one a hundred yards or so on the right. The moment we passed the second development, the curves lessened, and the road went straight. We passed two short columns of pine trees and wild brush that hadn't yet been cleared or filled in. Something huge, dark and towering loomed about half a mile straight ahead. Only a short line of flickering lights penetrated its enormous mass. I guessed that it was the hotel Mike had mentioned to me. The same hotel I'd been taken to by Johnny Grayson and his gang of thugs.

"Turn off your headlights," Mike said.

"No problem." I did as she said.

"What's no problem?" Neil gawked uneasily at me, then at the lights peppering the darkness straight ahead. "And why'd ya do that?"

"I think we're getting warm."

"Speak English, Deacon." Neil continued studying the row of lights in the dark structure awaiting us several hundred yards ahead. "What the hell's going on? Tell me. I deserve to know."

"Give me about a minute. Then I'll tell you what I think is going on."

181

We went down a short hill that leveled off and veered to the right. The parking lot out front was nearly deserted. Five vehicles were parked in darkness close to the front entrance. Lights illuminated three windows on the second floor. Other than that, the huge building appeared empty.

But I saw no sign of a gray van.

"I'd park on the far side of that pickup if I were you," Mike said. "You won't be able to be seen from the entrance, and the leaves from those palmettos out front will hide you from the windows that are lit."

I did as she suggested.

"And kill your lights," she added.

Once again, I did as she said.

"I'll be right back." Mike quickly vanished.

"What's going on, Deacon?"

"I told you I'd let you know."

"You told me you'd let me know in about a minute. Well, it's been a helluva lot longer than that already. Matter of fact, it's been more like two or three minutes."

"I honestly don't think it's been that long."

"I do."

"Neil—"

"Talk to me, Deacon. Right now. I mean it."

I sat back and took a breath. He was getting on my nerves. I kept reminding myself that we were friends. We'd been friends for several years. I also had to remind myself that, besides Phil, my ex-wife, Neil was the oldest friend I had.

In this case, I could sympathize with him. He was going through some serious hell right now and deserved a little compassion. True, I wasn't exactly the poster child for compassion, but I knew it wouldn't take much to keep the man under control. Mike would come through for us. I just hoped she'd come through quickly. While I was still thinking rationally.

"Well?" He was waiting for an explanation.

"About a minute could mean two minutes, Neil. Or three. Or maybe five."

"Dammit, Deacon, cut the bullshit. If this is some sort of stupid wild goose chase—"

"It isn't."

"Then why are we just sitting out here in the middle of nowhere, parked in front of a hotel that doesn't even look open? By the way, must I remind you that we're in Kissimmee? And that this isn't even my jurisdiction? In other words, I shouldn't even be here right now."

"You *wanted* to come with me. In fact, you practically forced your way—"

"That's not what I'm saying, dammit."

"I know."

"Deacon? Please give me a heads-up? Anything?"

"The van's parked out back," Mike said, appearing behind me. "And they're both on the sixth floor. Erin's being held in a small room. She's sitting in a chair and her hands are tied behind her back. She's hooded and scared to death. There are two men with her. One is watching the windows,

183

the other standing behind her with a gun pressed against her neck. I heard them say they're going to leave the room and take her downstairs and out back, then put her in the van. They've haven't said much else, so I don't know what they're planning to do once they leave the area. But my gut says this isn't going to be good for her. Also, I don't think we've got much time."

I pulled the Cheetah out of its holster under my arm.

Neil was watching me closely. His tiny blue eyes had grown enormous. "What the hell?"

"They're here," I said.

"You mean—"

"You packing?"

"Damn right I'm packing." He unclasped his .45 from the holster over his hip and jammed one into the feed.

"Then let's go get her."

"Deacon, how the hell could you possibly know—"

"Listen to me and do exactly as I say. Get Benton and whoever else you want on this. Tell her to get Kissimmee out here if you like. Just get them out here quietly. There's a gray van parked behind the hotel. In just a few minutes, two men are going to stick Erin in the back and take her away from here."

"How the hell do ya know all this?"

"My hunch."

"Yeah. You and that goddamn hunch."

"Does it matter how I get this done as long as I get it done?"

"Dammit, Deacon... If you're wrong about this—"

"Neil, just do as I say. Get them here *quietly*. That means no sirens, no lights—no nothing."

Glaring at me, Neil produced his cell. "Deacon, I gotta say—"

"Say it later. There's no time right now." I pushed the door open, slipped out and closed it quietly behind me.

***

The lobby was semi-lit.

No one was standing behind the desk. If they'd hired a desk clerk, he or she was either taking a nap or had retired for the night. I glanced at the door marked *STAIRS* but shot that down immediately in favor of the elevator. I was in no mood to manage six quick flights and engage in a gunfight in a corridor with a mob guy using Neil's niece as a shield.

"You're going to have to use the stairs." Mike had apparently read my mind again. "It's the only way."

"I don't want to risk getting Erin shot."

"You won't."

"You sure?"

"They're using them as we speak."

"Where are they?"

"Right now, they're on five, coming down fairly quickly. One of them is waiting in the van. The corridor's dimly-lit. You need to wait till they

185

get on this floor, which opens out into the rear parking lot. Cleaning supplies and laundry carts are blocking the way. They'll have to squeeze by two of the carts to reach the door. There's room behind the cart on the right for you to hide. The staircase is only lit on the second and third floors, so you won't be seen. He'll be much too busy getting the door open and keeping a firm grip on her to make sure she doesn't try to get away. In other words, he'll be concentrating on her. And the door. And since he thinks he's relatively safe here, he won't be expecting any surprises."

"Got it." I pulled out my cell and pressed Neil's number. "Neil, one of them is in the van. He's probably armed."

"Copy that. Benton's on her way over. She called Kissimmee, and they should be out directly. Her EST should be five minutes. Have you seen Erin yet?"

"Not yet, but I'm pretty sure I'm about to."

"I'm trusting you, Deacon…"

"I know."

"Please don't fuck this up."

"I won't."

"You're sure? I mean absolutely, positively certain about all this?"

"Not even slightly."

"Dammit, Deac—"

I pocketed the cell. Then hurried over to the stairwell door and eased it open slowly and carefully. I slipped through, inched it silently shut and got out my penlight. I could hear faint steps and some shuffling a few flights above my head. I gripped the gun in my moist, trembling hand. My pulse raced as I crept over to the set of stairs that led to the floor I was on.

***

There was ample room to allow me to hide behind the laundry cart.

Once I'd positioned myself, I gently pulled one of the garment bag carriers closer, until it was directly in front of the cart. The two empty garment bags hanging at the end of the rack hid me from view while the darkness did its job of concealing my exact location just a few feet from the rear door.

"I'm over here." Mike hovered somewhere on my left, between the rack and the stairwell doorway.

"You carrying?" I asked, attempting some humor to ease my fractured nerves.

"No, but if you hand me a gun, I can't guarantee that I won't drop it."

Despite the circumstances, I smiled. "I'm glad you're here, Mike."

"Concentrate on what you're doing. You can compliment me later, after we finish this."

Moments later, the shuffling of shoes on the concrete floor directly above me became louder. I gripped my gun and was relieved that the trembling in my hand had diminished.

The increased shuffling told me they'd reached the landing. The dark shapes moved closer. I could hear Erin moaning softly beneath the hood.

"Shuddup, bitch," muttered the guy with her as they moved closer to the exit door.

In just seconds, they were only a few feet away.

I kept my breath shallow and even. And braced myself.

A shift in the air quite close to my face told me someone was reaching for the doorknob just a couple of feet from where I stood. The instant I raised my arm, the shadow in front of me turned in my direction. The darkness was heavy, but he seemed able to see me, nonetheless. Or felt my presence. Either way, the result made my heart skip a couple of beats. Even in the dark I could see his eyes growing, filling their sockets. I watched in horror as his gun hand moved away from the shape in front of him and turned steadily in my direction.

Then, in that one intense moment of heavy silence, I heard Mike say, "Boo!" directly behind him.

He must have heard her, too. Cringing, he snapped his head in her direction.

I brought the barrel of my gun down sharply onto the top of his head. It came down hard, causing a dull, echoing *thump*! in the stairwell. Then, the instant before he began to fall, I grabbed his gun. He made a loud gurgling sound and dropped like a sack of potatoes.

I grabbed Erin by the waist and pulled her away just as the man collapsed onto the hard cement floor. The moment I grasped her, she tensed up and arched her back to get a good scream going. Since I was still holding the other man's gun, I used my forearm to press against the area where her mouth would be under the hood. I immediately felt the sharp ends of her teeth clamping down on my flesh. Gasping, I brought my face close. "It's me, Erin. Ralph Deacon. Your uncle's friend. The asshole's down and sleeping soundly. You're safe now. And you're turning my arm into messy strands of bloody meat!"

She sighed in relief. The pressure of her teeth immediately vanished. Then she nodded.

"You okay now?"

Another nod.

"Please. Whatever you do. Don't scream again, all right?"

She nodded one last time.

I pulled my arm away.

With a deep sigh, she fainted and collapsed in my arms.

Chapter 24

Neil looked pretty tired the next morning, when Mike and I went to see him in his office.

However, he acted much chipper and less angry than he'd been in days. His color had returned. The bags under his eyes had nearly vanished. He was moving around easier and acted more like himself. His tie wasn't even crooked or pulled down. And it looked like he'd finally remembered to shave.

"What's new?" I asked, sitting down in the chair facing his desk.

"The perp who broke Grayson's neck got away." Neil said it flatly, but he was obviously disappointed and frustrated by the whole thing.

"And you said the van had already left by the time you and Benton—"

"It just disappeared. The road behind the hotel circled back around and ended up back on one-ninety-two. It could be anywhere now, far as we know."

This was getting more annoying by the second. "Any chance Erin saw the man's face? If she could provide you with a sketch—"

Neil shook his head. He went over to the coffee station on the table behind his desk and poured coffee from the pot bubbling and spewing black vapors at the darkened wall behind it. He handed me a cup and sat down. "Hell, no."

190

"Not at all?"

"Now what fun would *that* be?"

"Yeah, we don't want things to get too easy, do we? It might make us lazy and complacent." As always, I placed the cup on the edge of his desk and sat back so the vapors couldn't melt my eyelashes or the hair in my nostrils. Mike said nothing, just made her usual face of disapproval.

"She said there was a guy Grayson talked to all the time they were working on you, but he didn't show until he came back to the hotel after he'd done Grayson. By that time, they'd already tied her up, stuck the hood over her head and planted her butt in the chair."

"Smart of them."

"Smart. And damn aggravating."

"I guess we don't even know who else was involved. Other than the two we caught last night."

"Well, as of fifteen minutes ago, neither were talking. We ran prints and mugs and found out a little about the one you slugged." He logged on and clicked through several screens. "Here he is, bigger than shit."

I got up and went over to Neil's desk. The thug I'd beaned was right there, his ugly scarred face filling the screen. Andrew R. Rokowsky. Age 41. 5'11', 210 lbs. Born in Tampa. Divorced three times. His list of offenses included petty larceny, embezzlement, battery, armed robbery, assault, and two charges of aggravated rape.

"No murder or other capitals in there?"

"One attempted, but it was dropped. He did a nickel at Stark out of a ten-year sentence."

"Good behavior?"

"Hardly. Looks like he had a bud in the right place."

"Where?"

"Seems a driver for Raguzzo got him off, somehow."

"Raguzzo? Really?" I was surprised.

"This was quite a while ago. Ten years, to be exact."

"Anything from the driver?"

"No, but the name Bergman came up."

"*Sonny* Bergman?"

"We questioned the big jerk, but it came up empty. Bergman said he never heard of Rokowsky."

"I'd be real surprised if he'd said anything different."

"We thought so, too."

"And not surprising. For a guy as big as Sonny, he can still manage to squeeze out of just about anything. I'm guessing you can't prove a connection."

"Good guess."

"Nothing else from the other guy, then?"

"No record whatsoever. An attorney working intermittently with Paseo Group Investments is on his way from Miami to talk to him. This tells us all we need to know."

"Vega."

He nodded. "But once again, we can't prove a connection. Not enough to implicate Vega in a court of law, that is."

"So then, we've really got nothing?"

"Just a couple of hunches." He gave me one of his accusing looks. "Although our hunches never seem to bring us the same results yours do."

I shrugged. "What can I say? I'm lucky that way."

"Yeah. Well, one of these days, you're gonna have to fill me in about these hunches of yours. And how they always seem to be right. And how they always seem to make total idiots out of the rest of us."

"Ask him about the Galvani guy," Mike said.

"By the way, you wouldn't happen to have a mug for Galvani, would you?"

"Why? It's not like you or Erin actually *saw* the bastard…"

"Humor me, okay? Call it an early birthday present."

"Your birthday's months from now."

"It touches me that you even remember that special event."

"Don't get silly, now." He sighed and pressed more keys.

A shot of a mean-looking dark-haired guy in his early forties with gaunt cheeks and jagged scars over his left eyebrow and on both sides of his mouth covered the screen.

"Satisfied?" Neil asked.

"That's him," Mike said, standing beside me.

193

"I'm satisfied," I said.

"You saying you saw this guy?"

"I didn't say that at all. I just said I'm satisfied."

"Then ya *didn't* see him?"

"No. I didn't."

"So why are we standing here like shitheads, looking at the asshole's pic?"

"Because I asked you to. And, of course, because we seem to be sharing a genuine moment together."

Neil groaned. "Deacon, you can really be a genuine pain in the ass."

"Thanks, Neil. By the way, you can turn that off now. I've seen enough."

Neil sat back and studied me in silence for nearly half a minute. "You're not gonna do anything stupid, are ya?"

"Define stupid."

Neil logged off and had a sip of the steaming battery acid. "Anything that'll get you in trouble with me. Or with anyone else involved in this."

I just shrugged.

"Deacon, I need a little more than a simple shrug."

"All right. How's this? I won't do anything stupid."

"Promise?"

"Yeah. Whatever." I stood and turned for the door.

"Where ya going?"

"Things to do, people to annoy."

194

He watched me for a few moments. Then, giving me his usual perplexed look, he said, "Do what ya do best," and had another sip of the steamy dark brew. "I guess we'll talk later."

"I guess we will."

***

Five minutes later, I sat in the TransAm, staring at the cell in my hand.

"What now?" Mike asked.

"I wish I knew."

"You have no idea what you're going to do next?"

"What makes you think I'm going to do anything?"

"You're holding your cell and staring at it."

"So…?"

"Every time you have your cell in your hand, you call someone."

"Good point."

"So? What's up?"

"I've got to make a call."

"Why aren't you, then?"

"I really don't like making calls like the one I've got to make."

"Why not?"

"It involves talking to some extremely unpleasant people."

"I think I understand. You're talking about those crazy Italian guys who run that strip club on the Trail."

I found it unsettling that she always seemed to know exactly what I was talking about. "How'd you know?"

"It's kind of obvious, isn't it?"

"I have to talk to a lot of unpleasant people in this business. It's part of the job."

"Then you should be used to it by now, right?"

"That doesn't mean I have to like it."

She didn't reply.

"Well?"

"You're right, I guess."

When I didn't comment on that, she said, "I have this strange feeling that something else is bothering you."

I shrugged. I didn't want to get into an argument with her right now.

"Does that mean yes? Or no?"

Her question told me that I wasn't about to be let off the hook so easily. "It means that I'd like you to tell me something."

"All right…"

"What I don't understand is how you always know what I'm about to do."

"You mean, like in this case with the cell phone?"

"That would be a good place to start, so let's go with it and see where it leads, okay?"

Mike nodded. "Well, you always look really nauseous when you're about to talk to those people."

"Seriously?"

"Look in the mirror."

196

I sat up and studied my face in the rearview. Sure enough, she was right.

"See?"

"Yeah." I sighed. Then I punched in the number for Vesper's Vixens.

"Want to give me a clue about this? Or should I try another guess?"

"Whatever suits you."

She started to say something, but I waved her down when I heard a harsh click in my ear.

"Vesper's," chimed an energetic, low-pitched female voice. "We specialize in the very best entertainment for the very best gentlemen in Central Florida. May I give you our lunch buffet special for the day?"

"No thanks. Unfortunately, lunch isn't an important issue for me today. I just need to talk to Sonny Bergman."

"May I ask whom I'm speaking to?"

"This is Ralph Deacon. Sonny and I—well, let's just say he knows who I am."

"And may I inquire about the nature of this call?"

"You can tell Sonny that I'd like to discuss a very urgent business matter with him."

"One moment, please…"

While I waited, Mike said, "This is about that Galvani person, isn't it?"

"You're a good guesser, Mike."

"This was easy."

"How so?"

"You can't use my ID to go after him. That is, unless you tell your rude police buddy about me. But even then, the police won't be able to use the ID. Since I'm dead, I'd guess that they wouldn't want to deal with a dead woman."

"You're absolutely right. Otherwise, this would be a slam-dunk."

"You think your mob boss friend can help you do this?"

"First of all, he's not my friend. Secondly—"

"Whaddya want, Deacon?" Sonny asked in his loud, abrupt voice.

"Nice to hear your voice, too, Sonny. And how are things? The family doing all right? You eating good?"

"Cut the crap. I'm busy here."

"I need to talk to Papa Joe."

A pause. "And what makes ya think I know where the boss is? I'm here. This is a big town. I got no fucking idea where the boss is."

I sighed tiredly. I often wondered if Sonny made me go through this sort of drill just to irritate me. I preferred to think that he just liked hearing my voice. Even so, I was in no mood for this.

"You just told me to cut the crap. I'm about to tell you to do the same."

"Deacon, you shithead, I'm about to hang up…"

"Go ahead. Hang up. When something happens very shortly to your place that will involve OPD, I'm sure Papa Joe will want to do a tap dance on

198

your thick skull for not getting in touch with him when—"

"What's this all about, Deacon? And what makes ya think I can get in touch with—"

"Three very important reasons. One, he owns Vesper's. Two, he lets you run the place, but only if you report to him on a regular basis. This tells me— along with anyone else carrying around a working brain cell or two—that you know exactly how to get in touch with him. And three, he told you not very long ago that when I need to talk to him, all I have to do is call you and tell him, and he'll take it from there."

Another pause, this time longer.

"Sonny? Still there?"

A heavy sigh. "Gimme a couple minutes."

Click!

I pulled the phone away from my ear, but not quickly enough.

"He doesn't like you, does he?" Mike asked.

I gently rubbed my ringing ear. "I prefer to think that he considers me a very formidable force of nature."

"One he has to deal with, but doesn't have to get to chummy with?"

"That more or less defines our so-called relationship."

"I'm glad he's not the clingy type."

"So am I. It makes breathing slightly difficult with a three-hundred-pound gorilla smothering you in a bear hug."

"You think that mob guy who isn't actually your friend but who thinks a lot of you will call back?"

"Papa Joe's mean, nasty, corrupt, and has done some really disgusting things in his long career. He's also not very nice. But he's always treated me all right. That is, he's been treating me all right ever since he tried blowing me up ten years ago."

"Don't forget that time he hired you to find out who was trying to take over his organization."

"I don't think he's forgotten that, either. Italians have long memories—especially when it involves someone who once did them a favor."

I heard a couple of rapid clicks. I figured it was Papa Joe's line being, as always, scrambled.

"You wanna talk to me, Deacon?" The old man's voice sounded even raspier and weaker than usual. I figured it was probably because he was rapidly approaching eighty. Or because the homegrown hot peppers he liked eating straight from the bottle while watching TV at night were tearing up what was left of his esophagus. It made him sound even more like the late actor, Robert Loggia.

"Hi, Papa Joe. How're things?"

"Things are just fine." Another *click*. "Sonny tells me ya need to talk to me about somethin' urgent. Is this urgent, Deacon? I hope for your sake it is. I'd hate it if this wasn't somethin' I'd be interested in."

"It's urgent. Very."

"Talk to me, then."

"I need to tell you something that will be of great benefit to your organization."

"Don't follow ya, *paisano*. Speak better English."

"This is about someone working for you who's been teaming up with someone from Vega's organization. This individual from Vega's outfit has obviously been teaming up against Vega in a dirty scheme that has gone bad. As a result, this whole dirty thing all might lead the cops to turn in your direction."

Silence.

I waited.

Another click.

"You sure about this, Deacon? I mean really sure? Positive?"

"You know me."

"Yeah. I know ya."

"Well?"

"You got a name?"

"Galvani."

Another pause.

"You did say Galvani, didn't ya? Ugly bastard from New York? No manners?"

"That sounds like him."

"Son of a bitch." A sudden silence. Then: "You're sure?"

"Positive."

"Tell me what else ya think's goin' on."

"Galvani was involved with a couple of Vega's men in the kidnapping of the niece of Orlando's Chief of Detectives. Galvani and his partner Johnny

Grayson kidnapped me and orchestrated an extortion scheme that went south when he broke Grayson's neck. It feels like some sort of power struggle, but we'll never really know. Incidentally, Grayson was the one who'd planned it. The scheme involved a mole working at OPD. Now that this has turned into a murder investigation, both OPD and the Kissimmee cops will be getting involved in it very shortly."

Silence. I knew that last tidbit would get him. Papa Joe hated having to deal with cops, lawyers or reporters.

"All right," he finally said, in a tired voice.

"I can't do anything on this end to keep you out of this. If I could ID Galvani, I'd definitely take it from here. You wouldn't even have to worry about this. But since I can't…"

"You're sure that *sfachim's* in on this?"

"Positive."

Silence. I could practically hear the gears grinding in the old man's head.

"You got it from here?" I finally asked.

"Yeah. I got it."

"You take care."

"You, too, *paisano*."

"I will."

"Deacon?"

"Yeah?"

"I owe ya. Big."

Click.

202

Chapter 25

Two days later, as I was having breakfast, Neil Haversack called to tell me parts of a body floating in Lake Toho had been found by the Kissimmee Police.

"Do you realize I'm having breakfast?" I wasn't interested in listening to the gory details while digging into my scrambled eggs, rye toast, and hash browns. I already knew what had happened in Kissimmee. But I also realized that it wouldn't be very bright to let Neil know that I knew.

I heard him sigh. "As a matter of fact, I didn't realize that. Some of us have to work for a living. Which requires us to show up at the office fairly early in the morning. Long before now, in other words."

I swallowed some egg and washed it down with my special brand of Jamaican coffee. "Tried that for a while. Didn't like it a bit. Messed up my tanning schedule."

Neil sighed. "Anyway, as I was saying…the body that was fished out of the lake wasn't much. Just most of the torso, an upper arm and both thighs—"

"Thanks for the image." I pushed my plate away.

"Gators, obviously."

"Thanks so much for sharing."

"Dammit, Deacon…"

"I know, I know. I guess we're talking about Galvani, right?"

A short pause. "How'd you know?"

"I'm a good guesser."

Neil paused. I could hear him trying once again to decide what was going on with me. "Actually, if you figured that one out so easily, you're a *great* guesser."

"I just figured that you wouldn't call about something like this unless it involved me or that last case we were working on. I *am* trying to enjoy my breakfast, you know. Something you apparently have already done, right?"

"Well, since I've been up since six-thirty, have showered and shaved, and since my gut has been full for at least an hour, I'd say that's another pretty fair assumption." He paused. "Yeah, Kissimmee thinks the local gators found themselves a special New York treat."

"Okay, since you obviously want to stay on the subject… A positive ID was made?"

"I wouldn't be calling if it wasn't—would I?"

"What were you able to get? A print? Dental?"

"No dental. The head was missing."

I frowned at the forkful of hash browns I was just about to spear with my fork. I dropped the fork onto the plate, pushed the works away again and covered it with my paper towel. "Thanks for ruining my breakfast, Neil."

"No problem. Anyway—"

"Galvani apparently crossed horns with the wrong gentlemen."

"The way it looks, he obviously tried to crawl his way back to the Raguzzo's and found out the hard way that they were waiting for him."

I sipped more coffee and tried to concentrate on getting my appetite back. "Sounds like a good scenario to me."

"Just one thing, though…"

"What's that?"

"How'd they know?"

"How'd who know what?"

"How'd the Raguzzo's know what Galvani was up to?"

"Your guess is as good as mine."

"You're not gonna tell me, are ya?"

"Tell you what?"

Silence.

"Neil?"

"Yeah?"

"Are you finished destroying my appetite?"

"For now."

"I would like to get through the rest of my breakfast before I go in to the office this morning."

"Morning? It's nine o'clock, dammit."

"It's morning until twelve. Then it's noon. It's been that way for a long time. That's why clocks were invented."

Another deep sigh. I could tell that he was about to hang up on me.

"Deacon?"

"Yes?"

"Thanks."

"For what?"

"You know what, dammit."

"I won't say it was a pleasure, but it's what I do, you know."

"I know."

"How's Erin doing?"

"According to her mother, she's been quiet since we took her home. It's gonna be a while before she's herself again, but I think the experience has taught her a valuable lesson."

"Any idea what they're considering charging her with? If you can get a good lawyer to keep her looking good as a kidnap victim, they won't be able to get nasty and pull a Patty Hearst thing on her."

"We're still on the fence about that. Jane's talking with an attorney I know, and they're working on something right now. Community Service has already been mentioned—that is, if we can keep her as the victim in this. We don't think Erin will quibble about something like that. Not after what she's just been through."

"Well, with Grayson and Galvani dead, who else could make her look good for conspiracy?"

"The only one who can say she was actually involved in this little caper is Rokowsky. But with his record, he's not exactly an eyewitness a jury with any normal amount of working brain cells would believe. If, that is, this even makes it to trial."

"By the way, did you ever find out who Galvani's blue contact was?"

"Benton's investigating that one for me. IA's already looking at one or two individuals involved closely with evidence coming into the Station. One of them already has a reprimand or two on his record. I'll letcha know what comes up."

"Sounds good. By the way, how much of that money do you want back?"

"How much have you got left?"

"I haven't figured it out yet. I didn't spend much of it. The motel rooms ate most of what I did spend."

"Keep it. It was money well spent. My sister also thanks you."

"Did you tell her it's what I do?"

"Actually, I didn't tell her much about you at all."

"Good. Keep it that way. She's much better off. And Neil?"

"Yeah?"

"Hang up. I'd like to finish my breakfast."

"Later, Deacon."

Click.

I pulled my plate back and slid the paper towel back onto the counter. Just as I snatched up my fork, I noticed Mike sitting on the stool beside me. "How long have you been there?"

"Just long enough to hear you tell your rude police buddy about the difference between morning and noon."

"How'd you like that?"

"It was all right, I guess."

"You guess?"

"I obviously have to keep reminding you that I really don't have to care about time anymore. Just when I'm working with you."

I ate a forkful of hash browns and forced myself to stop thinking about Galvani's bloody torso.

"They got him, didn't they?"

"Yeah."

Mike went pensive for a moment. "I don't really approve of such violence, but I also don't approve of people who run around, kidnapping and frightening people half to death."

"Well, Galvani's out of the picture now."

"And your mob buddy owes you a favor."

"Yes, but—"

"I know. He's not your buddy."

"Would a buddy try blowing you up?"

"I honestly hope not."

"There you have it, then."

Mike tilted her head, and her hair slid down her hazy shoulder. "I'm really glad you explain things so well to me."

"It's what I do."

"As I just said, you do it superbly." Mike smiled.

I had more coffee.

"What are you going to do after breakfast?" Mike asked.

"Go in to work. Why?"

"I just wanted to know if you'll still be needing me."

"I'll always need you."

"I'm talking about needing me this morning."

"Why? Got a heavy date somewhere in the Great Beyond?"

"No, but I do need to recharge. And wander. And do other things I can't tell you about."

"Just do me one more favor."

"Sure thing."

"Just don't stay away so long, okay?"

"Got you." She smiled. "Later." Then she vanished.

As always, I felt a heavy pang of sadness whenever she left me. Hopefully, she'd be back. And soon.

I didn't want to think about what I'd do if she didn't come back. I just finished my breakfast and the rest of my coffee.

And enjoyed what peace and quiet I'd have left before I got in the TransAm and drove to the office.

Other FUNNY DETECTIVE Books
By David Berardelli:

THE FUNNY DETECTIVE
"Taking on the Orlando Mob"
JUST A SIMPLE ERRAND
WORKING FOR A MOB BOSS
LOOKING FOR A DEAD GUY
HUNTING THE TALL BLONDE

Titles available through:
Fiction4All